1|9⁰

FIREFLIES

ALSO BY DAVID MORRELL

*Limited edition. With illustrations by R. J. Krupowicz.
Donald M. Grant, Publisher, West Kingston, Rhode Island.*

FIREFLIES

DAVID MORRELL

E. P. DUTTON NEW YORK

*Published in the United States by E. P. Dutton,
a division of NAL Penguin Inc.,
2 Park Avenue, New York, N.Y. 10016.*

Library of Congress Cataloging-in-Publication Data
Morrell, David.
Fireflies.
I. Title.
PR9199.3.M65F57 1988   813'.54   88-3588

ISBN: 0-525-24680-0

Designed by Nancy Etheredge

1   3   5   7   9   10   8   6   4   2

First Edition

Excerpt from "Sweeney Agonistes" in *Collected Poems 1909–1962*
by T.S. Eliot, copyright 1936 by Harcourt Brace Jovanovich,
Inc., copyright © 1963, 1964 by T. S. Eliot,
reprinted by permission of the publisher.

Excerpt from "Burnt Norton" in *Four Quarters,* copyright 1943
by T. S. Eliot, renewed 1971 by Esme Valerie Eliot,
reprinted by permission of Harcourt Brace Jovanovich, Inc.

This book is dedicated to the staff, nurses, and physicians at the University of Iowa's Hospitals and Clinics. One of the largest teaching and research hospitals in the United States, it exemplifies the best, in terms of both skill and humane values, that the medical profession ideally represents.

The nurses who administered to my son—in the Pediatrics Clinic, in the Children's Ward, in Surgery, in the Bone Marrow Ward, in Intensive Care—are too many to mention by name. Each did her or his part with utmost sensitivity and talent. My wife, my daughter, and I remember you with gratitude and love.

Of the physicians who cared for Matt, special thanks

are due to Drs. Raymond Tannous, Janet Graeve, Kevin Pringle, Roger Giller, Brian Wicklund, Michael Trigg, Robert Soper, C. Thomas Kisker, and Pedro De Alarcon. I apologize for any names I've missed. Those months were trying, and my memory sometimes fails me.

Thanks are also due to Cecilia Coulas, Diane and Michael Batty, Barbara and Richard Montross, Helen and Nicholas Rossi, and Gloria and Rudolph Galask, without whose compassionate support my family could not have endured what we sometimes thought could *never* be endured. Fathers Henry Greiner and Thomas Miller, true servants of God, provided the spiritual consolation we so desperately craved.

But finally, crucially, this book is dedicated to Matthew.

God love you, son. Watch over us. We did our best to watch over you.

Contents

Give sorrow words: the grief that does not speak
Whispers the o'er-fraught heart, and bids it break.

—SHAKESPEARE
Macbeth

Prologue
THE RETURN OF
THE ANCIENT MARINER

1

A well-known novelist acquaintance (I see him seldom but think of him fondly) once began a famous book with one of the most arresting passages I've ever encountered. The novel was *Ghost Story,* its author Peter Straub.

And this is how he started.

> *What was the worst thing you've ever done?*
> *I won't tell you that, but I'll tell you the worst thing that ever happened to me . . . the most dreadful thing. . . .*

Precisely.

I've borrowed Peter's words because they so perfectly express what I'm feeling. The worst thing I've ever done? I'll leave that troubling question for a different book.

But the worst thing that ever happened to me? The most dreadful thing? I can tell you that with absolute certainty. Indeed, with terrible compulsion, I find myself driven to describe that ordeal. My effort isn't voluntary. It comes in torturous rushes. Distraught, I remind myself of Coleridge's Ancient Mariner, in a frenzy stopping friends and strangers to tell of my woe, as if by describing it often enough, I can numb myself and blunt the words—and in so doing heal myself of the cause behind the words.

The effort's impossible, I suspect. Certainly, it didn't work for the Ancient Mariner. After killing a bird of good omen and enduring a consequent nightmarish sea voyage, he managed to return to shore.

> *Forthwith this frame of mine was wrenched*
> *With a woful agony,*
> *Which forced me to begin my tale;*
> *And then it left me free.*

Left him free? Well, apparently not, for Coleridge adds a marginal note that "ever and anon throughout his future life an agony constraineth him to travel from land to land."

> *Since then, at an uncertain hour,*
> *That agony returns:*
> *And till my ghastly tale is told,*
> *This heart within me burns.*

THE RETURN OF THE ANCIENT MARINER

I'm no more free than the Ancient Mariner. To be sure, I haven't killed a bird of good omen, though I recently saw a metaphoric version of such a bird die—and three days later I saw a literal bird, very much alive, that seemed to be a reincarnation of the departed soul of the first. A cryptic reference? You bet. Necessarily so, and soon to be explained. A mystical experience; and along with terror, sorrow, agony, guilt, compassion, God, and redemption, it's very much a part of my tale. For like the Ancient Mariner, my heart surely burns to tell you—once and for all, to be done with my tale, to exorcise my demons, to gain and preserve my faith.

2

Men fear death as children fear to go in the dark; and as that natural fear in children is increased with tales, so is the other.
—FRANCIS BACON
 "Of Death"

Fear. For almost twenty years as a fiction writer, I've focused on terror as my main subject. I've always believed, as Sartre in *Nausea,* that real life is so fundamentally boring that we need adventure fiction to help soothe our ennui, to take us out of the doldrums of actuality. The paradox, of course, is that if we ever truly experienced a "thriller," we would find it so terrifying we would wish with all the power of our being to be returned to the safe but depressing boredom of reality. T. S. Eliot puts it this way in "Sweeney Agonistes":

> *"I'll carry you off*
> *To a cannibal isle . . .*
> *Nothing to eat but the fruit as it grows . . .*
> *Nothing at all but three things."*
> *"What things?"*
> *"Birth, and copulation, and death."*
> *"I'd be bored."*

Bored? I don't think so. Not me any longer. For I have seen real life at its starkest. I've learned that copulation and birth have an unavoidable consequence: death. Despite what I used to think (and what Sartre thought), I know this much—that real life, whatever else it might be, isn't boring.

Because recently I was overwhelmed by a massive dose of my subject matter. I came face-to-face with terror, and now I have trouble writing thrillers. Having encountered death, I find that to write about it using the conventions of a thriller makes me feel I'm holding back, leaving out death's grisly secret. And yet to include that secret would be to negate the distracting purpose of a thriller.

So to tell my tale I've compromised. Most of what you're about to read is fact. I still can't believe it happened, but God have mercy, it did, and I feel an obligation to tell it. Since others have suffered as I and my family have, perhaps from our experience and the lessons we strained to learn, others will learn and find solace. In the aftermath of the tragedy we endured, we took great comfort in Harold S. Kushner's *When Bad Things Happen to Good People*. But the book you're now reading is different from Kushner's in many respects. For one thing, his excellent volume (though prompted, as was mine, by a personal tragedy) is a wide-ranging discussion of crises of faith that he encountered among troubled members of his synagogue.

For another, his book is totally factual.

However, *Fireflies* devotes itself exclusively to one family's tragedy, and though almost completely factual, it does have elements of fiction. Not the fireflies, the dove, and the other mystical experiences I will describe. I assure you they did happen. Still, because I wanted to make a statement about grief, about faith and the afterlife, I imposed a frame of fiction onto fact. In an epilogue, I'll explain where fact and fiction diverge. I'll also explain my reasons for blending the two, and my conclusion will, I hope, be spiritually rewarding.

> *Can I see another's woe,*
> *And not be in sorrow too?*
> *Can I see another's grief,*
> *And not seek for kind relief?*

> —WILLIAM BLAKE
> *Songs of Innocence,*
> "On Another's Sorrow"

TO FEAR TO GO INTO
THE DARK

1

Now he was old. One month shy of his eighty-fourth birthday. His daughter, Sarie, not so young herself, sixty-one, stood beside his deathbed in the shadowy, raspy confines of an isolation room in Intensive Care. Shadowy, because the blinds had been closed to ease the strain on his aching eyes. Raspy, because no matter how faint his hearing had become he couldn't fail to register the constant hiss, wheeze, and thump of the respirator thrusting oxygen down the constricting tube in his throat. No doubt there were odors—of medication, of his own diseased body—but he'd become so accustomed to the pungent, sick-sweet, acrid smells of the hospital that he no longer detected them.

Basically, David thought, I'm all fucked up.

Well, what do you expect? he told himself. You learned forty years ago—cancer's nobody's friend. And an old fart like you had to run out of resilience some time. Like five years ago. When your wife died.

But the true erosion of his spirit had begun much earlier, with the death of his son of fifteen years, on that night forty years ago when the cancer that now soon would kill the father had killed the son.

The circle was being completed. An agony of soul, a torture of spirit, produced by death would conclude with death. Matthew, the son for whom David had mourned all his life, would no longer be an absence beyond toleration, no longer a loss so profound that the passage of time intensified instead of mollified the pain. Grief, which smothered and swallowed, like a gathering black hole, would soon with damnable mercy end.

Death stops all hurt. Certainly David had tried to console himself with that thought in the first weeks after Matthew's death. At least my dear unlucky son's at rest, he'd repeatedly tried to assure himself. Matthew's six months of suffering, of chemotherapy, nausea, and Black-and-Decker chainsaw surgery had mercifully stopped.

But if Matt hadn't gotten the tumor, or if the chemotherapy had managed to work, if the surgery had been effective, he'd have survived. In that respect, Matt's death wasn't merciful at all. It was a vicious trick inflicted on a boy whose strength of character against panic and pain had made him truly already a man.

Death stops all hurt? You bet. It stops everything, including my son, David thought. And now when it's my turn, I don't care. Because I've lived my life, such as it was, and I'd have given anything to take Matt's place, because his love for life was greater than mine. Existence made him laugh, and my wonderful doomed son should have had the chance to continue laughing.

2

So David thought during his dwindling moments in Intensive Care. In his morphine stupor, he couldn't communicate his despair to the nurses who with stoic skill kept watch on his IV pumps, urine catheter, heartbeat and blood pressure monitors. He probably wouldn't have told the nurses anyhow, wouldn't have demeaned the purpose that *they* had managed to find in life, their solace in alleviating pain.

Nor could he have told Sarie, his sweet wonderful child of sixty-one, that she shouldn't grieve for his pain and impending death because *he* didn't grieve for himself. The pain didn't matter. It was no more than he expected. And as far as his death was concerned, well, that would be a release that over the years he'd many times considered granting to himself, though for the sake of his loving wife and daughter, he'd rejected that assault to their sanity.

Sarie stood over him, her face contorted with exhaustion, sorrow, and fear, using cloths soaked in ice to wipe his fevered brow just as he and Donna had with equal primal stress and devotion wiped Matthew's brow. Full circle. The daughter become the parent. The son become the father. And what did it matter? Love, in the end, was the greatest hurt. To love was to suffer loss— the more profound the devotion, the worse the grief. The noblest human emotion was fated to end in the greatest hell.

So David did his best to smile around the irritating oxygen tube crammed down his throat and to squeeze his daughter's hand in thanks. After all, he and Donna had raised her to value loyalty and compassion, and there was no need, at this late date, to disillusion her, to signal that he'd been wrong, to warn Sarie that love in the end brought loss and pain.

In his morphine delirium, David thought of his dead wife, Donna, and how much he missed her, not because she was beautiful as the fashion world knows beauty (though for all that, she'd been beautiful to him), and not because she'd been perfectly understanding and kind and forgiving (God knows she'd had a temper and could be maddeningly impatient and obstinate), but she'd been his companion for sixty-two years, and a couple— if they had the stamina to negotiate a long marriage— learned to make adjustments, to compromise and com- pensate, to allow, to tolerate. What it came down to was that both of them had reached a truce based on mutual protection, sympathy, and respect. Human imperfection and dissatisfaction produced a bond of pity and support. Neither husband nor wife could endure without the other's loving help.

But Donna had died, as all organisms must, in *her* case from a stroke, the fated consequence of lifelong hypertension. And how David had grieved, and how he had missed her. In his lonely bed, for the missed pleasure of merely holding her. At his solitary dinner table, for the absence of a conversation based on three-quarters of a lifetime of common memories over a mutually organized meal. But for Donna, death had been a matter of life creeping out its pace and finally reaching its unavoidable close. A monumental sorrow, but not a universe-tilting tragedy, not the wickedly untimely death of a tortured fifteen-year-old son whose talents and good nature had promised to improve the world. Death when it came to the elderly was understandable, a bitter natural order. But when a talented good-natured young man died, the cosmos showed its true malevolent identity.

3

So David thought as his daughter squeezed his listless hand, and his numbed body sank deeper toward oblivion.

"I love you," Sarie whispered. The remaining pride of his life, she'd had an existence to be envied, devoted husband, fulfilling career, no anguish, no serious illness in her or her husband or her children. The way it should have been for me, David thought. For my wife. For my son.

There once had been a year, the last before his son had died, when everything, every element of every day, had been perfectly aligned and rewarding. In every sense.

Creatively. Spiritually. Physically. Emotionally. Monetarily.

Perfection. And then an accident of the universe had struck, a cell gone berserk in the right sixth rib of Matthew's chest, and time had been measured accordingly—before Matthew's death and, God have mercy, *after* Matthew's death. Sarie, blessed daughter, had managed to adjust and mend. But not David and Donna. Effort had become the norm, pointlessness the rule.

Even now, after so many years, David vividly remembered, as if he were reading it this very minute as he was dying, the eulogy he'd written for the son he missed so fiercely, the son whose life had ceased with cruelty at fifteen and who'd left a vacuum never to be replenished. David had written the eulogy the day after Matthew's death. The priest hadn't known Matt and confessed he didn't feel qualified to make a consoling statement at the funeral.

So David, whose occupation was words, telling stories, had mustered the strength to decide that if words were the means with which he identified his place in the world, the least he could do would be to use what he did, to perform what he was, and try to make sense out of nature's lack of reason, to let outsiders understand Matthew's ordeal, and to strain for a moral lesson.

Alluding to a famous character he'd created (without ever mentioning the name of the character), he'd struggled to neither waver nor faint at the funeral, while he glanced dizzily toward the urn containing the ashes of his son—and the picture of his robust son in his prime.

16

4

"I'm a storyteller," he'd read at ten in the morning on Tuesday, June 30, 1987. "It's all I basically know how to do. For the first time in my life, I hate to do it, though. Nonetheless I'm going to tell you a story.

"Sometimes life kicks you in the teeth with an irony that a self-respecting fiction writer would be ashamed to invent.

"So it was that last November I began a new novel with a scene in which the main character seeks peace in a Zen Buddhist monastery in Bangkok where he meditates upon the four truths of Buddha.

"Life is suffering.

"That is the first of the Buddha's truths. It was also my first sentence.

"Life is suffering.

"As I finished typing those words at three-forty-five on a beautiful Thursday afternoon in autumn, I turned to glance out my study window and frowned at the sight of my fifteen-year-old son, Matthew, staggering across our front lawn. He was doubled over, his left hand pressed against his right chest. I rushed to meet him as he stumbled into the house.

" 'I can't breathe,' he said. 'The pain. There's something wrong with my chest.'

"No doubt I broke several traffic laws, speeding to our family doctor. Really, I don't remember. A lengthy exam made it seem that Matt had pleurisy, an inflammation of the lining of the lung. Antibiotics were prescribed. The pain went away.

17

"But as the Buddha says, *life is suffering.* During Christmas vacation, the pain came back, not in his chest this time but in his back. An X ray revealed that Matt had a tumor the size of two fists.

"And so the horror began.

"Matt had bone cancer, specifically a type known as Ewing's sarcoma. We hadn't detected it sooner because Ewing's is sneaky. The pain comes and goes. Often it isn't at the site of the tumor but rather at various other sites responding to presssure from the tumor. For a brief time, the explanation for the pain seemed to be that Matt had hunched over too long in marathon guitar-practice sessions.

"Ewing's is an uncommon form of cancer, but when it develops, it's usually in an arm or a leg. In this case, the uncommon cancer had chosen an uncommon spot, the underside of Matt's right sixth rib. Even so, Ewing's had been known to respond to chemotherapy. His chances of surviving were judged to be eighty percent.

"In January, he rapidly learned to familiarize himself with the names of arcane-sounding drugs. Vincristine. Methotrexate. Adriamycin.

"Cytoxan. The last part of that chemical's name—not its spelling but the way it's pronounced—says everything. Toxin. These substances were poisons intended to kill the tumor, but unavoidably they hurt healthy tissue as well.

"By early February, Matt's long curly hair, grown in imitation of his rock music heroes, had begun to fall out in huge disturbing clumps that littered his bed and clogged the drain when he took his morning shower. It's a measure of Matt's spirit that he decided to cut this

18

ugly process short by having a party in which his friends ceremonially shaved him bald. Some of them still have his locks. His eyebrows and eyelashes were less easy to deal with. He let them fall out on their own. He never tried to disguise his hairless condition. No wig for him. He displayed his baldness boldly for all the world to see and sometimes stare at and on occasion ridicule.

"It's a further measure of Matt's spirit that the weakness, disorientation, and vomiting produced by his medications never slackened his determination to persist at school. A straight A student soon was making grades that a few months before would have embarrassed him.

"But he hung in there.

"Chemotherapy was infused through an intravenous line, a tube surgically implanted beneath the skin of his left chest. You couldn't see it. But you could feel it. And for sure, every day, Matt was terribly aware the tube was present. The chemicals didn't take long to be administered, an hour for each, but their damaging side effects to the bladder required a prolonged irrigation of saline solution to flush the chemicals from his system. Thus the beginning stages of Matt's treatment forced him to stay in the hospital for three days every three weeks and to recuperate at home for another three days. A small price to pay.

"Except that after several applications, it became frighteningly manifest that the treatment wasn't working. The tumor had continued to grow. More aggressive chemotherapy was called for. His survival chances were now fifty percent. But as the weakness, disorientation, and vomiting worsened, he still didn't lose his spirit. He began to think of the tumor as an alien within him, a monster whose strength, intelligence, and will were pitted against his own.

" 'But I'll beat it,' he would say. 'I'll win. I want to be a rock star when I get older.'

"Life is suffering.

"The more aggressive chemotherapy didn't work either. His physicians moved from chemicals that under ideal circumstances gave cause for hope to agents that are called 'investigational,' that is they'd been used so seldom that permission from the hospital's ethics committee was required before Matt could receive them. Nonetheless, of the twenty-two cancer patients who'd received them, eighteen had experienced dramatic results. Sounds good. But you don't receive investigational therapy unless you're in the twenty percent of patients predicted to die.

"Again Matt familiarized himself with arcane names. Ifosfamide. Mesna. VP-16. Now, in April, the length of his stay in the hospital while receiving chemotherapy was *five* days every three weeks. And the hangover from these drugs took another five days. Between treatments, he had only eleven good days, if 'good' is a word that applies here.

"For once, the treatment worked. The tumor shrank fifty percent. Imagine his elation.

"Imagine his equal and opposite distress when the next time he received these chemicals, the tumor—the alien—adjusted to them and began to grow again.

"Surgery was the only option. In late May, four right ribs and a third of that lung were removed, along with the tumor.

"Or rather most of it. Because the alien had spread

seeds, and to kill them, the doctors had to use even more aggressive treatment. A pint of Matt's bone marrow was extracted from his hips. A tidal wave of chemicals was infused, enough to kill all his white blood cells. His healthy bone marrow was returned to him. Eventually it would produce healthy blood. All things being equal, he would regain well-being. The cancer, viciously assaulted, would be killed.

"But all things weren't equal. Normally harmless bacteria in and on his body bred out of control. No longer held in check by his usually vigilant white blood cells, they stunned him with a rampant infection known as septic shock. The top number of his blood pressure plummeted to forty. His heartbeat soared to a hundred and seventy. His temperature surged to one hundred and five.

"But he hung in there. Antibiotics killed the bacteria. Conscious though struggling against an oxygen tube in his throat, he used a trembling finger and an alphabet board to spell frantic words of conversation. Morphine was used to ease his struggles against the oxygen tube. He was last conscious a week ago Sunday. But even after that, he reflexively gripped the hands of sympathizers with unbelievable strength. Until last Saturday evening, when after eight days in Intensive Care and six months of unremitting ordeal, something in him wore out.

"Life is suffering.

"Only Matt knows how much he suffered. His mother and I, his sister, his relatives, his friends, his teachers, his nurses, his physicians, all of us can only guess. Because he never complained, except to ask 'When

21

am I going to get a break?' And even then he'd add, 'But I'll beat this damned thing.'

"Maybe he did. Maybe the cancer would never have come back. In the end, not evil cells but normally innocent ones defeated him. As I said at the start, life's ironies can sometimes kick you in the teeth."

David had trembled at the lectern in the church. After another agonized gaze toward the urn containing Matthew's ashes—and the photograph of Matthew in his long-haired robust prime—David had dizzily faced the mourners and struggled not to faint.

"What I've just described to you was hard to write and more hard to say. But I didn't do it out of perversity, out of some horrible need to make you feel my hurt. And his mother's hurt, and his sister's, and that of all the rest of you who were close to him. I did it because there were many who saw only the carefree, good-natured, happy-go-lucky pose he bravely demonstrated to his associates. Many had no idea, not the faintest notion, of what he was going through. He wanted it that way. And he succeeded. He even successfully completed his ninth grade of school.

"His spirit, his bravery, his humor, his determination ought to be models to us all. Life in the last analysis indeed is suffering, but the lesson Matt gave us is that pain and disease can destroy us. But they need not defeat us. The body in the end must die, but the spirit can endure."

David had paused again, trembling, struggling not to faint. Through tear-blurred eyes, he'd mustered strength to focus on the swirling words of the text he so fiercely wished he didn't have cause to recite.

"When prolonged unfair disaster strikes, the obvious question is why? I read in the newspaper about mothers who strangle unwanted newborn infants, about fathers who beat their children to death, while we wanted so desperately for our own child to live. I ask why can't *evil* people suffer and die? Why can't the good and pure, for Matt truly was both, populate and inherit the earth?

"If we view the problem from a secular point of view, the unwelcome answer is simple. Disregarding religious solutions, we're forced to conclude that there is only one cause for what happens in the world. Random chance. Accident. That's what killed Matt. A cellular mistake. A misstep of nature. If so, we learn this as well. Given a precarious existence, we ought to follow Matt's example and prize every instant, to make the most of the life we've borrowed, to be the best we can, the bravest, the kindest. For at any moment, life can be yanked away from us.

"There are those who would have lapsed into hedonism, into alcohol, drugs, and other forms of reckless self-indulgence. That was not Matt's way, for he worshipped creativity. Strumming on his guitar, dreaming of a career in music, he knew with a wisdom far beyond his years that beauty, good nature, and usefulness were the proper values.

"But from another point of view, a religious one, we learn something else.

"Life is suffering, the great Buddha says. That was his *first* truth. He had three others.

"*Suffering is caused by the wish for nonpermanent things. All living things die. Everything physical falls apart.* That was the Buddha's second incontrovertible truth.

23

"And the third? *Suffering ends when nonlasting things are rejected.* No person, no object, no career can finally bring happiness. In a world of eventual destruction, only eternal goals are worth pursuing.

"Which leads to the Buddha's fourth and last great truth. *Seek the eternal. Seek the forever-lasting. Seek God.*

"Matt wasn't religious in the sense that he belonged to an organized body of faith. He was baptized as a Roman Catholic. He was trained in that religion to the point of what Catholics call the sacrament of Communion. But to him every other religion had value as well. He did believe in God. He wore a small crucifix as an earring. On one of his last conscious days, he received what the Catholic Church used to call the sacrament of Extreme Unction, the final rites, what it now calls the sacrament of the sick. We know Matt's body was sick beyond belief, but I assure you his soul was wholesome to its depths, and I'm convinced the sacrament spiritually and psychologically eased his passage.

"Poor dear Matthew, how we grieve for him. But in addition to his hopes of being a musician, he had three final wishes, which I'll share with you.

" 'If I die,' he said, 'I want to be surrounded by a communion of my friends.'

"Today, with love, we've achieved that wish for him.

"His second wish?

" 'If I die,' he said, 'please remember me.' With all the tears in my heart, son, I swear you'll be remembered.

"And his third wish?

" 'I hurt so much,' he said. 'I want mercy.'

"My unlucky wonderful son, in a way I can barely

adjust to, you received that wish also. You did gain mercy.

"Sleep well, gentle boy. Be at peace. We'll think of you with fondness till we ourselves pass. And if there is an afterlife—I confess I'll never be sure till I find out—I know you'll forever be in loving tune with us.

"Say hello to Jimi Hendrix for me. John Lennon. And Janis Joplin. All the other departed music greats. Pal, I bet you've got a hell of a band."

5

So David had read at his son's memorial service. Next to him on the altar, beside the photograph of a glowing son and an urn filled with ashes, had stood Matthew's favorite guitar, a white combination acoustic-and-electric made by Kramer, the instrument Donna had purchased for Matt the day of his extensive surgery. Waking from sedation after being monitored in Intensive Care, not yet knowing that the cancer had not been fully removed, he'd been shown the guitar and, too weak to hold it, had managed a tearful grin of joy, his weak voice breaking. "Isn't that beautiful?" David, about to die now forty years later, still heard those heart-choking words reverberate through the morphine swirl of his mind. His son had survived to play that guitar only four muscle-weary times, discouraged because his fingers no longer retained their skill.

In the eulogy, David hadn't included the further

agonies his son had endured. After the chaotic heartbeat, respiration, temperature, and blood pressure that were part of the septic shock, Matthew's kidneys had failed. Dialysis had been required. Not the kind in which a machine is used to filter poisons from the blood. That type of dialysis couldn't have prevented Matt's failed kidneys from causing excess fluid to accumulate in his body. Choosing a different method of dialysis, a surgeon had desperately slit open Matt's abdomen and inserted a tube through which liquid was poured, its special properties establishing a correction of blood chemistry by means of a process called osmosis. The liquid sucked not only poisons but excess fluid through Matt's abdominal lining, and every hour that poisoned fluid was drained, replaced by a fresh solution. But the poisons and excess fluid had resisted treatment, not leaving his body quickly enough.

Then Matthew's left lung had collapsed. Then his muscles had begun to contract from lying motionless for too many days. Donna and David had put on and taken off his socks and sneakers every hour to prevent his Achilles' tendons from tightening. Finally dead bacteria from his septic shock had collected within his heart. A chunk of this debris had broken from within the heart and plugged a main artery. Death after eight days in Intensive Care had not been from cancer, but instead from a heart attack. Ironies. How they kick you in the teeth.

So David thought as he came closer to death in Intensive Care. Even now, after forty years, he remembered the autopsy report that he and his wife had received.

Dear Mr. and Mrs. Morrell:

On behalf of the physicians and staff at the University Hospital, I extend our sincere sympathy at the loss of your son. This letter is to inform you of the preliminary results of his autopsy.

1. History of Ewing's sarcoma with no gross residual tumor identified. Detailed analysis reveals no evidence of malignancy. (*David's translation: The treatment worked. The cancer was cured.*)

2. Status post bone marrow transplantation: successful. Healthy blood had begun to generate. (*Translation: If Matthew hadn't succumbed to septic shock, he'd have been home within a few days, on the way to complete recovery.*)

3. Endocarditis, an inflammation of the lining of the heart, with abnormal tissue deposits on the valves of the heart. (*Translation: Debris from the dead bacteria.*)

4. Complete blockage of the left main coronary artery. (*Translation: The effects of the treatment, not the disease, were what killed him.*)

5. The lungs were heavy in weight and fluid, consistent with respiratory distress syndrome. (*The oxygen pumped into Matt's lungs to keep him breathing would eventually have poisoned his lungs.*)

6. The kidneys were swollen. The outer layers were pale, consistent with damage due to septic shock. (*If his heart hadn't killed him, his kidneys might have.*)

7. The bladder was inflamed and hemorrhagic. (*How much can a poor kid withstand?*)

8. Both the stomach and the esophagus had ulcers. (*Why not? Everything else had gone to hell.*)

9. A cerebral aneurysm was present in one of the vessels in the brain, an abnormal dilation of the blood vessel. He also had small areas of bleeding along the lining of the brain. (*Sure, the consequence of the septic shock, and if the cancer hadn't killed him and the heart attack hadn't, maybe with Matthew's bad luck, he'd have had a stroke.*)

10. The liver was found to be enlarged. (*Might as well throw that in. The chemotherapy was extreme, all right. After the removal of four ribs and a third of a lung, he wasn't strong enough to bear any further stress.*)

If you have any questions, please call [the letter concluded]. Sincerely . . .

7

David did have one question. How can life be so cruel? But the question at bottom was philosophical and an inappropriate response to an autopsy that proved his point empirically. Things fall apart. The center cannot hold. Watch out for the boogeyman. Eat your Wheaties. Say your prayers. Walk around ladders. Brush your teeth after every meal. Stay away from the teddy bears' picnic. And count every second without pain or disaster as a major stroke of luck.

Entropy. That was the secret. The messiness of the universe.

As Sarie held his weakening hand in Intensive Care, David heard faintly, through the wheeze of the oxygen pump and a humming in his ears, the words she'd recited at Matthew's funeral. How proud he'd been of her that day, how filled with love. The strength and composure she'd mustered against intolerable grief had made it possible for her somehow bravely to stand before the mourners at the church and to recite that day's gospel, a text that with bitter irony happened to be from St. Matthew.

Sarie repeated it to him now. God bless her, she'd remembered the passage all these years. She spoke it again as she had with the same trembling voice combating sorrow so long ago. If he'd had the strength, he'd have reached up and hugged her just as he had before the mourners in the church so many years ago when she'd stepped unsteadily down from the lectern. The words were beautiful.

> Come to me, all you who are weary and find life burdensome, and I will refresh you. Take my yoke upon your shoulders and learn from me, for I am gentle and humble of heart. Your soul will find rest, for my yoke is easy and my burden light.

Comforting thoughts. If a person believed.

But David at best had been an agnostic.

Until three incidents made him suspect there might be a spirit within the universe, a greater power than his pessimism allowed.

8

The first had occurred one night after Matthew's death. Having somehow managed the strength to write Matthew's eulogy, David had staggered to the master bedroom, where in a rare gesture of obeisance to a God whose existence he doubted, he'd sunk to his knees. The time was night. The room was dark. David's eyes were raw with tears. Hands pressed to his swollen face, he'd prayed with a fervor that he swore would kill him.

Matthew, Matthew, *Matthew!* I want you back, son! This has to be a nightmare! Soon I'll waken! You'll be here!

One day before the septic shock that had ravaged Matthew's body and eight days later killed him, David had used some brief time alone, when he and Donna weren't sharing anxious hours together watching over Matthew in the hospital. David had driven home to change clothes. On impulse, based on a twenty-year daily habit, he'd decided to exercise, to run as was his custom, to clear his head and sweat tension from his body. After four miles, the farthest he could manage given his stress and weakness, he'd staggered into his kitchen, sipped a glass of water, and collapsed. Surely while he was passed out on the floor, this nightmare of his dear son's death had come to him, and he hadn't wakened yet. That was the explanation. None of this had happened. It was a nightmare.

So he'd hoped forty years ago as he'd knelt in trembling anguish beside the bed. While he squeezed his hands to his face and tears seeped through his clawlike fingers that threatened to tear his cheeks away, he'd prayed with all the desperation his soul could sustain that he would wake up from his stupor on the kitchen floor and his son would still be alive.

Oh, please! he'd prayed. Oh, Jesus, please!

But he'd known in a terrifying recess of his remaining sanity that he had indeed revived from his stupor on the floor, that he had indeed staggered back to the hospital, that his son had indeed suffered septic shock one day later and died eight unimaginably traumatic days after that.

Matthew! Matthew! Please! Come back to me!

Forty years ago, in his kneeling paroxysm beside the bed, his thoughts flashing through his mind like lasers, David had suddenly remembered yet another example of his wonderful son's promising gifts. Not only the life-affirming pulse of music, whose throbbing chords continued to reverberate like a neverending tape through David's head, but as well a poem, one of many, this one written during the disorientation and nausea of chemotherapy, a poem that Matthew had later submitted for an assignment at school.

Fifteen years old. With verbal gifts far superior to those of his father who defined himself by and made his living out of words. Fifteen years old, and in a panic at 4:00 A.M., the boy had wakened Donna, who slept beside him on a cot in the IV-stand-filled room, to dictate to her his sudden terrifying insights. A poem. Not linear, not rhymed and metered, not the singsong unintentional parody of a poem you'd expect from someone his age. Instead a gestalt of fear and memory. A jumbled synthesis of reaction to when life was perfect and then collapsed. A metaphor of a jigsaw puzzle, of each piece

31

having been beautifully assembled and then perversely ripped apart; of lost hair, fading friends, and fractured hopes; of the prejudice ignorant people showed toward cancer patients whose bald heads and gaunt cheeks looked like skulls; of dreams become tears and parties about to turn into wakes. Death and a jigsaw puzzle. If the poem wasn't perfect, it was better than the father could have written at fifteen, or maybe could have ever written, and if a perceptive reader paid it due attention, the meaning was clear; the craft matched the content.

9

JIGSAW

Remembrance of the days of ecstasy.
A natural buzz from life was created
As every piece of the jigsaw puzzle
Was prime and in place.

A sledge hammer, chain saw, and a rototiller
Shred through the jigsaw puzzle,
Through the good memories
Of a lot of Cokes
And late night burgers.

A mane of hair,
A symbol of what you believe in.
And so many good times gone by . . . Gone.
Déjà vu rings strong in your ears

But brings not a smile to your face,
Instead tears to your eyes.

Prejudice rears its ugly head.
Social matters become shattered.
Limits are put in place.
The jigsaw puzzle is slowly destroyed.
Leaving only one piece . . . Alone.

10

Fifteen years old. Vomiting at 4:00 A.M. Dictating a poem.

God love you, son, David had sobbed on his knees, hunching over a bed, with his fingers like claws scraping into his tear-ravaged face. You *are* dead. I'm not unconscious on the kitchen floor. I'm here. I've just written your eulogy. And my existence, never content to begin with, will be forever empty until my own death.

A remarkable occurrence took place then. Fireflies filled the dark bedroom. They seemed to blink, and yet their light was constant, like flaming balls from Roman candles; but Roman candles dwindle in brilliance and flash in a straight-line arc, whereas *these* lights zigged and darted, zagged and swirled. They spun at the same time they soared. The room was ablaze with them, and David thought of them as fireflies because of their random dashing radiant pattern.

Fireflies. Splendrous! Of varying colors but all of equal magnificence. Rushing with the energy of joy.

Ecstatic. A swirling cluster of what David intuited beyond any question were rapturous souls.

He made allowance for his grief and stress, his weariness and shock. He wasn't thinking clearly at the moment, he readily granted. But the brilliant colorful fireflies were spinning and zooming before him, so patently real, so vivid, that he couldn't dismiss them, couldn't reject their beauty by denying the exquisite vision allowed to him.

Whether they were a hallucination or a visitation, he gave in to them and embraced their rapture. Of the thousands, among their myriad flashing colors of joy, he identified one in the cluster who he knew beyond doubt was his son. How he was sure, he couldn't tell. But that he *was* sure, he had absolute faith.

"Matthew, come to me."

For no reason he could account for, the spinning specks of flying fire reminded him of children in a playground, of his son as a toddler laughing and racing among other children. And just as Matthew when a toddler had been reluctant to leave the exuberance of his friends, so the darting firefly (no different from the swirling others but who the father knew with total certainty was Matthew's soul) refused to come to his grieving father.

"Matthew, I'm telling you! Get over here!"

But still distracted, continuing to revel in incomprehensible gaiety, the soul of the son ignored the father.

"Matthew, don't disobey me! I want you back! Get over here!"

At that, responding to the desperate insistence of the father who loved him beyond measure and mourned to the limits of sanity for his son's absence, the firefly that was Matthew's soul soared away from his satisfying companions, sped to within a foot of his father's weeping eyes, halted abruptly, and hovered for an instant, suspended in time.

"Dad, I want to play. At last, I'm having fun," the firefly soundlessly said, the inaudible words echoing within the father's head. "Don't you understand? I don't hurt anymore. I'm at peace. I'm where I belong. I'm okay. You've got to understand that. I'm *okay*. You hurt, and I'm sorry. But there's nothing I can do. You'll have to deal with it. I know how much you love me. If you didn't grieve, that'd mean you didn't love me. In that sense, grief is good. It hurts, but it's *good*. It's a tribute, and I love you for it. Grieve for yourself, for your emptiness and loss. As long as you understand I'm okay. I love you too, and I miss you. But it's not your time to be with me. Please, if you truly love me, Dad, let me go back and play."

With a sob that wracked David's soul, he nodded, and the firefly that was Matthew sped back to his swirling lights of friends. And with that, the vision ended.

The fireflies disappeared. The bedroom returned to darkness.

Kneeling beside the bed, sobbing with a greater sense of loss and yet a strange kind of joyous understanding, David slumped in exhaustion, then slowly, wearily, stubbornly stood. Because there were footsteps and voices from beyond the bedroom door, friends and neighbors, acquaintances come to offer food, respects, and condolences, and their gestures of compassion couldn't be demeaned by being ignored.

That had been the first of the three signals David

received, making him suspect there was a mystical property in the universe.

11

The second experience had occurred one evening later. It hadn't been as dramatic as the first, but for all that, it had been affecting and in its way profound. This was on Monday. Matthew had died on Saturday; the eulogy had been written and the fireflies had appeared on Sunday. But now it was Monday, the evening of what is politely called the visitation at the funeral home.

In this case, the visitation had not involved a view of Matthew's corpse, for David and Donna had agreed that a thorough autopsy had to be performed on the frail, scarred, pain-twisted remains of their wonderful son, who wasn't Matt anymore anyhow.

"Examine his body every way you can," David had said through scalding tears to the physician who signed the death certificate. "Take him apart. Learn everything you can. Perhaps what you discover will save some other poor kid's life. Do so thorough a job that there can't possibly be a public viewing. His body's yours."

"Thank you," the physician had said. "We appreciate your understanding. Sometimes commiseration for the family—and respect for their attitudes toward public viewing—prevents us from doing as complete an examination as possible and learning as much as we can."

"Some meaning has to come from this," David had said, so dizzy he'd feared he'd collapse. "To keep this from happening again, to crush this fucking disease. Ewing's sarcoma. It isn't just cancer. It's evil. It's the Devil. Sometimes I think we didn't need physicians. We needed an exorcist."

So there hadn't been a public viewing of Matthew's remains. But not just because of the thorough autopsy. For the second reason wasn't scientific but aesthetic. A corpse filled with formaldehyde and prettied-up with cosmetics to make the dear departed look lifelike, sort of, but not really? Spare me, David had thought. Ashes to ashes. Dust to dust. Never mind formaldehyde. Matthew had already been injected to saturation with too many chemicals.

So Matthew was cremated. His fifteen-year-old ashes filled a bronze container the size of a coffee grinder. According to local law, David, Donna, and Sarie could have done virtually anything they wanted with the urn. They could have taken it home and placed it on the mantel or stored it in the stereo cabinet or opened it and sprinkled Matthew's ashes onto a flower garden— just so long as they didn't dispose of the ashes in a public waterway or on public grounds.

But the mantel and the stereo cabinet seemed too morbidly remindful, and the flower garden—for all its natural appeal—would have prevented David from transporting Matthew's ashes if the family ever decided to move. No, to keep the ashes in the urn and then to place the urn in a mausoleum was the only acceptable option in a totally *un*acceptable force of choice. At least in that way, mother, father, and sister could be close (but not *too* close) to the beautiful son and brother they'd lost.

The visitation showed mourners the urn; next to it, a photograph of Matthew in his long-haired glorious prime; and next to that, on a stand, Matthew's seldom-played Kramer combination electric-acoustic guitar. Hundreds arrived. One heartbroken well-meaning youth brought a plastic bag filled with the light brown hair—already falling out from chemotherapy—that Matthew had told his friends to shave from him. The well-wishers, the mourners, the friends and loved ones at the vigil had been appreciated but emotionally draining. At the sight of Matthew's hair crammed within the plastic bag brought by Matthew's friend, David had nearly fainted. But two of David's friends had escorted him from the mortician's and driven him to the church where the funeral next day would occur.

That was where the second mystical experience took place. Donna and Sarie had been going through their own emotional strain, sustained by relatives who helped them to the church. At nine o'clock on a beautiful dusky June night, the family had entered the church. There were arrangements to be made, a funeral to be planned. In the end the music the group selected was "*Pie Jesu* (Merciful Jesus)," from Andrew Lloyd Webber's sad sublime *Requiem,* which he had written in honor of his dead father.

Stooped, barely able to maintain his balance if not for the supporting hands of his two friends, David had managed to enter the shadowy church. As he shuffled up the main aisle, his unsteady footsteps echoing off pews and rafters, his tear-reddened nostrils widening to the redolence of incense, flowers, and scented candles from that morning's mass, an eerie change went through him. A strength of solace, of well-being and reassurance suddenly grew within him.

For a second time, he heard the echoing voice of the firefly. It rephrased its words from the night before in the bedroom. "I'm okay, Dad. I'm sorry you hurt, but your grief is the proof of your love for me. Mourn for your loss, but don't mourn for me. Because you can't imagine how happy I am."

David abruptly straightened. He no longer needed his friends to hold him upright. With a strength that came from spiritual assurance, he approached the front of the church, where family and friends who watched him said afterward that he seemed different more than in manner, almost as if he had a glow.

He didn't feel better. His grief was as agonizing as before. Nonetheless he stood straighter. He could function. For he knew beyond doubt that his son was at peace, or in the firefly's word, "okay."

That I can handle, David thought. I can manage to suffer. For myself. If my son sends a message he's okay, I can strain through grief for myself.

Because I don't matter.

That was the second experience.

12

And the third? Twelve people saw it. All were astonished. None ever forgot it. As a witness later said, "It's getting harder to be an agnostic."

This is what happened. When the funeral service concluded, David stood and put his arms around Donna and Sarie. Sobbing, struggling to muster dignity and not stumble or faint, they left the church, followed by several hundred mourners.

That Tuesday morning was hot and bright. Blinking after the shadows of the church, David, Donna, and Sarie sat in a limousine whose white seemed incongruous yet appropriate because innocence—though dead—did not merit black.

The mourners remained outside the church, in grieved confusion. Three relatives and two very close friends got into the limousine as well. The representative from the mortician brought Matthew's urn, his photograph, and his guitar from the church. She set the urn on Donna's lap, then drove the limousine from the church, followed by the priest.

After Donna held the urn for a while, she handed it to Sarie, and as the limousine neared the cemetery, Sarie handed the urn to David.

It was heavier than he had expected, not because of the ashes, which for a frail boy had to be slight, but because of the bronze—possibly fifteen pounds. It was square, a shiny deep brown, and by now someone had taped a lock of Matthew's light brown hair to the top. On opposite sides of the urn, at the bottom, two screws secured the lid and what it contained.

Entering the curved gravel driveway of the cemetery, David noticed the groundskeeper, or what's known as the sexton, standing at the open gate. The man (who, David later learned, had once been an economics major and had never dreamed he'd make a thirty-year career of overseeing a cemetery) got into his car and led the limousine past seemingly endless, flower-topped graves toward a mausoleum at the rear of the grounds.

The mausoleum (the only one on the property) was not at all like the dingy box-shaped structures you often see in cemeteries. Instead it was peaked, made mostly of light-colored wood and stone, and resembled a chapel. Its front door was open. As the sexton stopped his car ahead of the limousine, David, Donna, Sarie, and the others got out to join him. All told, counting the sexton and the representative from the mortician, there were ten now. Then the priest arrived, and another representative from the mortician, and there were twelve.

"I normally keep the mausoleum locked," the sexton said, "but I wanted to ease your grief and avoid any awkwardness, opening the door and all that, so I could make this as smooth as possible for you. Later I'll give you a key, so you can visit your son's remains whenever you like."

Stifled tears. A murmur of thanks.

So the procession of twelve, led by David carrying the heavier-than-expected urn, stepped into the mausoleum that resembled a chapel. Inside, on the right and left, there were niches for coffins and urns, but straight ahead were chairs like pews, and an organ and a podium. The large rear wall was glass from top to bottom, with

41

sunlight pouring in. And David, who entered first, his tears dripping onto the urn, was the first to see . . .

What to call it?

A startling coincidence? A supernormal event?

What David saw was a bird. It flew around the chapel, soaring, swooping, circling, flapping in panic.

Recovering from his surprise, David turned to look past Donna and Sarie toward the priest, who followed through the open door.

David, who needed a respite from sorrow, a mitigation of grief, said with bitter irony, his humor black, "That's all we need, Father. The Holy Ghost."

But the priest stopped rigidly, reacting neither to irony nor to black humor. Indeed the expression on his face was a combination of shock, disbelief, and reverence. His face paled. "But, David, look closer! *It really is a dove.*"

That statement might not make sense to non-Catholics. In the Catholic Church, the Holy Ghost is a term that describes God's ability to inspire as well as console, and traditionally the Holy Ghost is symbolized by a dove.

That's what David—and the priest, and Donna, and Sarie, and the rest of the twelve—were seeing now. A dove. Not white, as in religious paintings. But gray, its name appropriate, a mourning dove, so-called because of its dirge-like "coo," so much like a sob. It flapped and swooped and soared.

"My God," the sexton said, not intending to sound religious. "I'm terribly sorry. I deeply apologize. I left the door open to make it easy for you to come in, but I should have thought. Sometimes a bird flies in if the door isn't closed. I'll try to get the dove out right now."

David shook his head, his black irony irrepressible, and anyway the service was all that mattered.

"No, leave it," he said, scanning the crypts to his right and left. "This place could use some life."

The sexton narrowed his eyes. "You're sure?"

"Absolutely."

The sexton and the mortician's representatives relaxed.

David found out later that an accidental interruption of the service, a distraction such as the dove, sometimes spurred mourners into fits of indignation, into accusations about insensitivity and incompetence.

Everybody's different, he thought. In his own case, he welcomed the dove. In fact, in a strange way, he even loved it. For its life. Let it flap and swoop and soar. As long as it doesn't hurt itself. When Matthew's in his niche, we'll take care of the dove.

The service began. As yet, there was nothing mystical, nothing supernormal about the dove. The door had for convenience been left open. The dove—as coincidence can happen—had by chance flown in. Perfectly explainable. Not usual, but nothing remarkable.

So far. But then coincidence was added to coincidence until, for David and the other eleven witnesses in the mausoleum's chapel, the dove became very remarkable indeed.

As the dove continued flapping, David set the urn on the podium at the front of the chapel. He, his family and friends, along with the sexton and the mortician's representatives, stepped back to the pewlike chairs. They watched the priest put on a vestment, then open a prayer book and begin the final liturgy for the dead. "Heavenly Father, accept this soul of your faithful departed servant . . ."

Throughout, the priest kept glancing nervously from the urn containing Matthew's ashes toward the dove flapping overhead.

Then the next coincidence occurred. As the priest neared the end of the prayers, the dove, which till now had been in a panic, suddenly calmed and settled from the ceiling toward a low ledge on the wall of glass.

The priest held his breath, directed an even more nervous look toward the dove, and resumed his prayers.

There's no way to verify what went through David's mind just then. He later swore to those in the chapel that he knew what would happen next, or at least that one of three things would happen.

The dove will land on the floor beside the podium that supports Matthew's urn, he thought. Or the dove will land on the urn itself. Or the dove will land on my shoulder.

David knew this as certainly as he'd witnessed the fireflies and heard one in particular in the bedroom two nights before, as certainly as he'd felt an unaccountable repose and heard an echo of the firefly's voice in the church the evening earlier.

The priest opened a vial of holy water, and the first thing David had imagined occurred. The dove flew down to the floor beside the podium.

The chapel became very still. The priest's voice fell to a whisper as he prayed and sprinkled the holy water over the urn.

The service came to an end. For several instants, no one moved. David felt strangled.

"After you leave," the sexton said, his voice soft with respect, "I'll put your son's remains in his niche, and then I'll remove the dove."

"No, we'll do it right now."

"I beg your pardon?"

"I want to be here when the urn's put into the niche," David said. "But first I'll take care of the dove."

"No, you don't understand. It's in a panic. It'll be difficult to capture," the sexton said.

David's brother-in-law added, "I'll take off my jacket. Maybe we can throw the coat over it and capture it."

"That won't be necessary," David said. "No need to worry."

The sexton frowned. "Then how are we going to—?"

"It's very simple. I'll pick up the dove."

"You'll *what?*"

"Oh, sure," David said. "Just watch."

For that had been David's final precognition. The dove would let him pick it up.

"Impossible," the sexton said.

"I told you, watch."

For David was already moving, neither fast nor slow, but steadily, with calm. The dove, its feathers ruffled in panic, darted its frantic eyes right and left toward corridors of escape, but remained where it was.

David stopped, and though the dove flapped its wings with brief uncertainty, it stayed in place.

David eased his hands around the dove. It didn't struggle.

David stood and faced his eleven witnesses.

"And now I'll set Matthew free."

He carried the dove past the urn, past his family and friends, and approached the mausoleum's sunbright open door. Outside in the radiance of what otherwise would have been a splendid June morning, he smiled at the dove, though his tears made the gray bird misty to his eyes.

"Matt, I hope you meant what you told me the other night. With all my love, I want you to be okay."

Reluctantly David opened his hands, and if the previous eight minutes had been packed with strange events, there was one more yet to come, for the dove refused to fly away. It perched on David's open palms and, for fifteen seconds, peered at him.

David almost panicked. His thoughts could not be verified anymore than his precognitions could. Nonetheless he swore that this is what he thought.

My God, when I picked you up, I hope I didn't hurt your wings.

At that, the bird soared away, its feathers making the distinctive whistling sound of a mourning dove in flight. It sped straight out, then up, ever higher, toward the brilliant sky, toward the blazing sun.

And was gone.

That's it, an inner voice told David. That's the last sign Matt'll give you. Three will have to be enough.

David felt pain, yet joy. The significance of the dove having lingered in his open palms he took to be this: the extensive surgery that had removed Matt's four right ribs and a third of his right lung was like picking up a dove and breaking a wing. But the dove had been all right, and as the firefly had said, so was David's son.

Matt was at peace.

In the days, weeks, months, and years that followed, whenever David returned to that mausoleum, he scanned the grounds in hopes of seeing the dove, praying for another sign from his son.

But he never saw it. He saw robins, blue jays, and sparrows. Never any doves.

That day, the sexton unscrewed the glass pane of a two-foot square niche in a wall. David handed the urn to Donna, who handed it to Sarie, who then handed it back to David, who kissed it, placed the urn in the niche, and watched the sexton replace the glass pane.

The ritual had ended. Time was now measured differently.

Before Matt. After Matt.

As the group left the mausoleum, David turned to the priest. "At the risk of sounding . . . I've got the feeling something spooky happened in there."

"David, to tell you the truth, I feel a little weird myself."

The group drove back to the family home, where the several hundred mourners had been invited. Because Matthew had asked for a party if he died, the largest, most animated his parents could arrange, with music, food, soda pop, beer, and anything else that would make the kind of celebration they'd have had if he'd survived. A few months before his death, Matt had prepared a demostration tape of his guitar skills. That tape was played a lot that day. So was music by Matthew's favorites: the Beatles; Van Halen; Bon Jovi; Crosby, Stills, Nash, and Young. And all through the mournful party, the priest and everyone else who'd been at the mausoleum couldn't stop talking about the dove.

13

When you lose a child (and you truly loved that child and weren't just an indifferent caretaker or that scum of existence, a brutalizer), you search for some meaning, some justification, anything to ease your agony. You think about God and whether He exists and what kind of God would allow something so heinous as Matthew's death. You think about ultimates, about the point of existence and whether there's an afterlife and what it would be like. Would Matthew be waiting when his father, mother, and sister died? Would he be the same?

You question everything. You grasp at anything. To make sense of what seems to have no sense. To find meaning in what you despair might be the ultimate meaning: nothingness. You seek in all places, all cultures. You search in all philosophies and faiths.

Reincarnation? Plato believed in it. For that matter, a full half of the world's present population believes in it. In the East. As the theory goes, we struggle through various stages of existence, not always human, sometimes animal or even plant, rising until we've perfected our spirit sufficiently to abandon material existence and join forever in bliss with God.

A complicated but comforting belief. Because there's

a point to life, a payoff. Certainly it's easier to accept than the notion that God tortures us here on earth to punish us for our sins so we'll be happy with Him in Heaven. In that case, how do we explain the death of an infant, who couldn't possibly have sinned? Or the death of a fifteen-year-old boy, who by all accounts was remarkable and never harmed anyone?

Matthew was a child with a wisdom beyond his physical age. At school, he'd become the envy of his fellow ninth graders because he'd been adopted by those in grade twelve. He ate lunch with the older students (unheard of). He went to grade-twelve parties (unheard of). He gave them advice about the problems in their lives, and (unheard of) the older students heeded his advice.

There was something about his character, his humor, his intuition that set him apart. Uniqueness by definition is one of a kind, and Matthew by all reports was indeed a breed unto himself. At school, a type of unfashionable student known as a nerd might be victimized by cruel remarks and equally cruel antisocial jokes. But Matt would put a stop to it all.

"Give him a break. If he's truly a nerd, if he was born that way, then let him be what he is, because *you* weren't born so unlucky. And if he's a nerd for other reasons, because of family problems maybe, all the more reason to give him a break—because he does have problems."

Matt's ability to grasp mathematical, philosophical, and verbal skills at school was astonishing. Instinctively. With minimal effort. Perfect grades. A Presidential scholar. In Iowa, where the test of basic skills is one of the standards of the nation, Matthew ranked within the top 1 percent of the most-gifted students.

And he never had to try. He budgeted his time for assignments at school as a necessary tedious inconvenience. His achievements seemed as effortless and natural as putting a record onto a turntable, as remembering. "Trailing clouds of glory do we come / From God, who is our home," Wordsworth says, the title of his poem appropriate: "Intimations of Immortality."

The transmigration of souls. Passing from one existence to the next, we accumulate in wisdom so that, no matter our physical problems, our spirit and intelligence grow stronger. Maybe so. David had often thought that Matthew was a mature man at eight. Matt's sense of fairness and justice, of virtue and honor, was astonishing at so early an age. He passed through stages more quickly than any child David had ever seen, and David had once worked as a counselor to adolescents. Before his death, Matt had—unbidden—been studying Oriental philosophy and its theory of reincarnation. Could it be that Matthew's soul had reached its prime, and the disease of his body, his soul departing from it, was like a butterfly leaving a chrysalis? Had Matthew's death not been a tragedy but part of the natural order? Such were the desperate thoughts that a grieving parent used to find solace.

Desperate thoughts. Nonetheless comforting.

But they didn't assuage David's loss, and after the funeral, after the party, the torture still hadn't ended. Because he, Donna, and Sarie each day had to enter Matthew's room, itself a black hole of absence, to stare at the clothes in his closet, the games on his shelves, the phonograph records on his bureau, the rock-star posters on his wall. The last day of school, Sarie and a friend had gone to Matt's locker to bring home his bag of notebooks, texts, and gym shoes. Sorting through that bag, and his closet, and his bureau drawers was an agony so extreme that it had to be done in stages, a little each day for weeks and months.

What do you want to save, what to throw out? How do you dispose of the vestiges of a treasured life? Matthew's tapes and records, collected over the years, had mostly gone out of fashion. His friends didn't want them. The posters on his walls came from a culture changing so rapidly that even those purchased six months ago might as well have been sixty years old. Those posters and rock-star buttons and banners were valueless without the perspective of the mind that had attached significance to them. Souvenirs have no worth without nostalgia, after all. They're meaningless if a memory isn't linked to them.

So once each week, David carried a plastic bag of the remants of a departed life out to the street and walked *far* from home so he wouldn't see the trash collectors take those bags away. Old shoes, still redolent of Matthew's smell. Socks and underwear, too personal for anyone else to put on. Stacks of bank statements, five dollars withdrawn on one day, seven dollars another day, a lifetime of withdrawals, until the ultimate withdrawal. The useful items, Matthew's clothes, were given to Goodwill.

At the last, what remained were three albums of photographs showing Matthew as he grew to his final year, and a pair of slippers shaped like bear's feet complete with claws. How he'd grinned as the nurses kidded him about those slippers, when he pushed his IV stand for exercise down the hospital corridor. Those slippers—too precious to be discarded, their smell of Matthew too comforting—were tacked to a wall in his room. And that was that, the conclusion of the disposal of what once had been a life.

Except for a final gift. One of Matthew's closest friends had moved far from town several years before. Each summer they'd taken turns flying to visit one another. Matt's friend had lost his mother to breast cancer, and one evening when the boy, delightfully sixteen with his life ahead of him, had phoned to keep in touch and say how much he missed Matt, the boy had added that his home had been burglarized, all his rock-music records stolen. The next day, all of Matt's tapes and records, nearly one hundred of them, were mailed to Matt's friend. How satisfying a gift, not so much for Matt's friend, though he surely appreciated the package, but satisfying for David, Donna, and Sarie. Because they knew how Matthew would have been delighted to please his friend.

What finally remained of Matt's possessions was the bright white Kramer electric-acoustic guitar that Matthew had treasured more than anything else he owned.

That precious guitar (polished frequently, with reverence) stayed in Matthew's room, almost like a holy object, supported upright on a stand, and each day, mustering a face to meet the faces that he met, David entered Matthew's room and stroked that guitar. For luck and strength.

"Help me make it through the day, son. And especially the night."

15

Time is the greatest healer—so David had been told. Untrue. Parents who lose a valued child never get over the dear one's absence. As David aged, he, his wife, and his daughter continued to cherish one another (a blessing, for too often the death of a child produces a split within a family: arguments, recriminations, and divorce). Except for terrifying anxiety attacks that imitated coronaries and eventually required psychiatric therapy, David's health was perversely good. His career as a writer prospered. The famous character he'd created (sometimes reviled, sometimes revered, but never ignored) took second place to other of his characters, who because of the sorrow David had suffered from Matthew's death spoke to readers who suffered their own sorrows.

He prospered. He persisted. But he did not flourish.

Maybe that was the final irony. David's unwanted success could have been a boon to Matthew, could have eased Matthew's way, through David's contacts, into the world of influence.

16

So David thought as he lay in a stupor, dwindling toward his own death, his faithful loving daughter beside him holding his weakening hand in the shadowy raspy confines of an isolation room in Intensive Care. His exceptional wife had died five years before him, and he'd grieved for her, how much so, but never the spirit-burdening grief he'd felt for Matthew. His wife, he knew, would understand. When Matthew had died, the world had shrunk. Everything afterward had been like climbing an endless flight of stairs.

God?

Heaven?

Reincarnation?

Who knew?

But now he was near the top of that wearying flight of stairs, and he'd discover the answer or he wouldn't, depending on whether there *was* an answer or merely oblivion.

"I love you," Sarie said.

Weak, struggling against the oxygen tube in his throat, David nodded. He knew she understood that he loved her as well. He was proud to have been not just her father, but her friend.

You were a gift to me, David thought about Sarie.

Just as Matthew was a gift, and it's too bad we're not all here together. Years ago I almost killed myself. Now I'm glad I didn't. Because of you, dear.

But now you'll have to go on without me. The main thing is, *my* death isn't a tragedy. My dissolution is part of the natural scheme. Grieve for me, because you love me, but don't let my death hold you back. Persist. And maybe one day, we'll meet in rapturous reunion.

Who knows? Good-bye, sweetheart. I pray I'm about to meet Matthew. I've missed him so much. If death is oblivion, it won't matter because I won't have the consciousness to know.

But if . . . !

Sinking ever deeper into the ultimate sleep, David's dwindling consciousness managed a final burst of strength. As if it were yesterday and not half a lifetime ago, he remembered another poem that Matthew had written, one that David had memorized with a persistence close to mania and could never have forgotten even on the verge of death.

The poem had been written when Matthew was fourteen. Imagine. So young. And it represented everything that Matt's young heart had wanted.

To be a musician. To be in tune with the spheres.

17

LOWDER
VOLUME
CO.

The guitar. Rubbing the gentle polish
On every smooth contour.
On the lap. Knowing every curve
As the light shines from it.

(Silently strumming)
On stage a planned metamorphosis
Takes places as the hours go by and the
Space is transformed to a concert hall.
The energetic nemesis has struck.

The risers are transformed into a stage
And black boxes turn into powerful
Pieces of sound equipment.
The spring is taut.

(Silently strumming)
Backstage while pandemonium
Sweeps the hall and people
Crowd the arena as ants flow to a cake.

The stage is set, the
Instruments tuned and placed.
The musicians work out last minute
Kinks as the lights dim.

(Striking power chords)
An intense force hits the spectators.
Energy is released in every form.
A power rage beyond comprehension.

Fourteen years old, and to have written a poem so promising of future achievements.

Gone. All lost and gone.

Sinking.

Dimming.

Dwindling.

And yet . . .

And yet . . .

In David's mind, he seemed to rise above his dying body, to float above his soon-to-be corpse, to see his daughter sobbing over him and the nurses rushing toward him, raising the bottom of his bed.

David knew what raising a patient's feet meant. He'd seen it happen to Matthew. When the nurses raised the bottom of your bed, your blood pressure was dropping, and you were, to use Matt's words, in serious shit.

So what did it matter? David's time had come, and he looked forward to it, hoping he'd reencounter a great love of his life, be replenished from his greatest loss.

In his mind, he floated ever higher, through the ceiling, and higher yet, away from the shadows into a brightness, drifting toward it, toward a door that somehow didn't interfere with the beautiful brightness.

When David's stepfather had suffered his first heart attack, the weary man had wakened to describe a dream in which he'd been floating through brightness toward a door.

"I reached the door. I knocked and knocked. But no one answered."

Three months later, when a second heart attack

had completed the job, maybe the tired man had reached the door and this time his knock had been answered.

But David didn't need to knock. Floating to the door, he merely turned its knob. At once he heard power chords. An electric guitar strummed ecstatically.

David opened the door. The brightness increased its glare; the strumming chords became more powerful.

The brightness he saw was caused by fireflies. Millions of them. Radiant. All around him. Enveloping. Silently rejoicing.

The chords throbbed with greater intensity. David peered all around, squinting past the fireflies.

Matthew? David's joy became frustration.

Matthew? Doubt became despair.

The radiant fireflies swarmed around him. But he recognized none of them!

Matthew?

Where was Matthew?

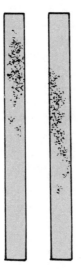

A POWER RAGE
BEYOND COMPREHENSION

1

Fireflies swarmed. Power chords throbbed. David opened his eyes. Sunlight gleamed through a window. Through a swirl, he saw a cupboard above him, the edge of a sink, a stack of dishes. About to vomit, managing not to, he turned his aching head to the left and saw the blur of a kitchen table. His movement bumped an object and sent it rolling.

David strained to clear his vision. He recognized the rolling object, an empty glass that the turn of his head had sent clinking to a stop against a leg of the table.

His hair was soaked. He lay in a pool of water. But his body was drenched with more than water. Sweat. His bare legs, arms, and chest were slick with perspiration. His shorts clung sweat-soaked to his groin and hips. *What was going on?*

Through misty vision, he focused on the digital clock on the microwave to the left of the table: 12:55.

A calendar (the kind you tear a page off each day) showed . . .

It couldn't be.

1987?

June?

Thursday?

The eighteenth?

Impossible! The last moment he'd known had been sometime in March. The delirium of morphine and the distracting pain of his mortal illness had made him unsure of the date. But without doubt he'd entered Intensive Care in March.

Forty years from now. So what was he doing on the floor of the kitchen of a house that he'd sold a year after Matthew's death because he couldn't bear the memories of . . . ?

A year after Matthew's death? *Intensive Care forty years later?*

With tingling feet and hands, David raised his head from the floor and peered at his body.

No wrinkles in his stomach. No cancerous gauntness in his chest. He was struggling through nausea to stare at the daily-exercised body of a man of forty-four. Despite his nausea, he felt in the middle-aged prime he'd known and then lost after Matthew had died.

After Matthew had died? June eighteenth? One day before Matthew had contracted the septic shock that eight days later had killed him?

62

Power chords kept throbbing. David squinted through a kitchen archway toward stereo cabinets against a wall in the living room. Lights glowed on a tape player. Stereo speakers thrummed. He still saw the fireflies, but now he realized that they were specks of lights inside his head.

His dizziness lessened. His memory cleared. He'd spent all night at the hospital, sleeping next to Matthew's bed. Donna had taken her turn to sleep at home, then had come up to the Bone Marrow Ward to trade places with David, to give him a chance to go home, shower, and change his clothes. He'd arrived home at eleven and decided to exercise, to run as was his custom. Frustration had made him run faster than usual, to sweat out his tension. But excessive humidity had added to the ninety-degree temperature, making it the equivalent of one hundred and three. Perspiring worse than usual, he'd stumbled into the house, turned on the tape player, poured a glass of water, raised it to his lips, felt dizzy, seen fireflies, dropped the glass, and fainted on the kitchen floor.

David realized that none of the other things had happened. Matthew's septic shock, his eight days in Intensive Care, his eventual death had only been a nightmare caused by unconsciousness due to overexertion and excessive loss of bodily fluid.

A nightmare.

Gaining more strength, David groped to his knees, crawled to the table, and tugged himself to his feet. For a moment he wavered. But with both hands on the table, he held himself steady. The fireflies dimmed.

Sure, a nightmare.

Then why had everything he'd dreamed appeared so real, as if the events of the nightmare had truly occurred and what he now saw was merely an illusion?

The power chords kept throbbing.

Why, if he'd merely fainted, was he so terrifyingly sure that on June twenty-seventh, nine days from now, his son would die from unexpected complications due to his cancer treatment?

The tingling in David's arms and legs made him wobble. He strained not to faint again.

Something was horribly wrong. He recalled the fireflies in his bedroom and the dove in the mausoleum.

But none of those things had happened!

Yet he knew, as if remembering, every dismal instant he'd endure for the next forty years. His future was so clear and detailed that he could not believe those forty years, every wretched minute of them, could have been crammed into so brief an unconsciousness.

While unconscious had he imagined the possible course of his life?

He breathed deeper, faster, on the verge of hyperventilating.

Or was he remembering his life from the perspective of forty years later?

His chest felt tight. *What in God's name is happening?*

In his dream, the next events in his life had been that, after he wakened from fainting, his dizziness had worsened. He'd been forced to stay in bed until the next day. When he felt well enough to return to the Bone Marrow Ward, his son had contracted septic shock.

But none of that had happened! At least not yet.

But *would* it?

His dizziness intensified. In a rush, he pulled a chair from the table and slumped into it. He propped his elbows on the table and clutched his head. His chest felt squeezed.

I'm having a heart attack!

But he didn't feel a sharp pain down his left arm. And his heart—though it rushed—didn't skip or feel stabbed.

Mouth parched, tongue swollen, he knew he shouldn't move if this *was* a heart attack, but he took the risk and staggered toward the kitchen sink, where he turned on the tap, bent down, and gulped water. He shoved his head beneath the faucet and drenched his hair.

At once, he had the vertiginous sensation of floating over an old man in a hospital bed. The old man's eyes were closed. Hooked to life-support systems, the old man was surrounded by nurses and doctors raising the foot of his bed, injecting medications, and turning dials on a respirator. An elderly woman slumped over the old man, sobbing.

My nightmare!

Drifting down a brilliant corridor, he hovered in a radiant doorway.

Fireflies.

Power chords.

Hunched over the kitchen sink, David almost threw up. Man, you're in really bad shape. You'd better go to bed.

But that's what happened in my nightmare! And the next day, the septic shock hit Matthew and . . . !

Septic shock? He suddenly realized he'd never heard those words before. Except in his nightmare. But he understood what septic shock meant. Or thought he did.

Floating from an old man's body. Hovering in a radiant doorway. Searching for a firefly among splendrous millions.

You'd better get control.

David drank more water and turned off the tap. Grabbing a dish towel, he wiped his dripping hair.

Well, there's an easy way to convince yourself it's all in your head, David thought. In your nightmare, before you staggered to bed, you phoned Matt's room at the hospital. You let it ring ten times, but no one answered.

David groped past a window toward the phone on the kitchen wall. Heart racing, he pressed the numbers for Matthew's room. One ring. Two rings. Ten rings. No one answered.

He let it ring longer. *Still* no one answered.

Feeling suffocated, David set down the phone. He pressed his back against the wall and strained to keep his knees from collapsing. In his nightmare, the explanation for the lack of response on Matthew's phone was that Donna had helped Matt get out of bed and walk into the ward so Matt could reach a bathtub in a room around a corner down the hall.

Again David floated.

He couldn't ignore his terror. He felt so sure of what would happen next that he had to act as if it *would* happen.

If he was wrong, he'd be grateful beyond belief.

But what if he was right? He didn't dare dismiss

the possibility that he'd been granted the gift he'd prayed for in his nightmare.

To dial back. To retreat in time. To take the knowledge of the future into the past.

Based on what he'd dreamed, given what he'd learned from his experience with Matt in Intensive Care, from conversations with doctors who reconsidered the choices they'd made, from conclusions based on the autopsy report, he had a precious opportunity.

To save his son's life.

2

The University of Iowa's hospital administers to patients not just in Iowa City but throughout the state. There are other hospitals in the area, of course, but few are so well-equipped to deal with extreme diseases, especially those involving children's cancer. A helicopter is available to fly emergency cases from hundreds of miles away. Other patients—chronically ill but not in imminent danger of death—sometimes spend hours being driven to the hospital for specialized treatment.

Two years before, when the demands of writing assignments had forced David to resign from being a professor of American literature at the university, he and his family had considered moving to another locale. Thanks to the famous character he'd created and the income he received from best-selling novels about other characters, he had the financial ability to live anywhere he wanted. After all, to work he needed only a word processor and a quiet room. He could set up those conditions anywhere. Los Angeles had been a likely place—because of the movie producers David sometimes worked for. New York City (or nearby in Connecticut) had also been an option—because he'd be close to his publishers.

But in the end, as a consequence of the many business trips he had to take, the palm trees he saw in California and the skyscrapers he saw in New York had begun to seem ordinary. Flying home, peering down at the rich black soil and rolling wooded hills of Iowa, he'd gradually decided that the Midwest was as exotic as any of the so-called glamorous sites he'd visited.

A friend had once laughed at David's choice of word. "Exotic?"

"Well, attractive anyhow, and more important, innocent. The air's clean. There aren't any traffic jams. I've never had to worry about my children being mugged in the schoolyard. I can get anywhere in town in fifteen minutes. The people are friendly. I like the space, the big-sky feeling. I guess what it comes down to is, I feel at home. I've settled. Even on a practical level, the dental and medical care are magnificent."

Medical care? Another irony, for David could never have guessed how desperate he soon would feel about the medical care he'd so praised or how fortuitous his choice to remain in Iowa City would be. Patients in the farthest reaches of the state had to travel hundreds of miles for their treatment. But David's desperately ill son could be driven to one of the nation's finest hospitals within five minutes; the family home was only ten blocks away.

The hospital is huge, much larger than most medical facilities even in major American cities. The complex stretches over blocks and blocks. New buildings are constantly being constructed. And some of the sophisticated diagnostic instruments (a magnetic resonance imager, for example) aren't available in many areas.

Yes, David thought, if your son gets a rare form of cancer and the tumor lodges where it almost never does—in a rib instead of an arm or a leg . . . if your son might have the only case of its kind in the nation, it's a damned wise choice you made in deciding to stay in Iowa City.

These thoughts occurred to him as he pushed away from the kitchen wall. With an unnerving sense of viewing everything from a distance, he staggered downstairs to shower, then stumbled upstairs to his bedroom, where he struggled to dress. Still dizzy, he knew he was risking a traffic accident by driving to the hospital, but the alternative, that of staying in bed till tomorrow as his nightmare had told him he otherwise would, was an unacceptable option.

He had to save Matt's life.

Driving carefully from the residential area, turning left toward the expansive towers of the hospital that it seemed he hadn't seen in forty years, he entered a parking ramp, where he found a place to leave his Porsche 912 near the Plymouth Voyager his wife had driven to the hospital. For a moment he leaned against his car to establish his balance, then walked as steadily as he could from the ramp to one of the many entrances to the hospital.

His mind was playing tricks on him. He felt unfamiliar with an institution that he'd visited almost daily for the past six months, as if he hadn't been here for half a lifetime instead of just this morning. Pushing open a door, he walked along a corridor that he'd gone down a thousand times and yet seemed barely to remember. He reached a large open area in which chairs surrounded a grand piano that doctors sometimes played during lunch hour. Plants hung from gleaming mirrored walls and a ceiling four stories high.

Turning right, he forced himself along another corridor, this too familiar but only as if through a mist. He reached an elevator marked G, and while it swiftly rose, he endured a powerful pressure behind his ears. With his hands cupped to his head to reduce the pressure, he heard an increasing hum within his brain.

What's happening to me?

His arms and legs now tingled so severely it seemed as if electricity stung him. The band around his chest squeezed tighter. His forehead felt cold, yet sweaty.

At the third floor, the elevator door opened. He lurched out, turned left down another corridor, and compelled himself not to waver. He even managed to quicken his pace.

Passing patients' rooms, he reached a nurses' station whose design seemed primitive compared to the type he'd seen in his nightmare.

"Mr. Morrell, how good of you to come back." A blond nurse smiled.

David remembered her, and yet it didn't seem from recent conversations, instead from long ago. "Come back?"

"We were hoping you'd give us a visit. How's Matt doing?"

"What do you mean? That's what I'm here to find out."

"But you know he isn't here. He left a week ago. He's up in Bone Marrow."

Oh, my God, David thought. I reached the wrong floor. I went to where Matt always used to get his treatment: the Pediatrics Ward.

From a child's room, he heard the distinctive sound of a nurse gently paddling her hands on the chest of a cystic fibrosis patient, clearing fluid, helping constricted lungs to breathe.

"Of course," David said. "I must have . . . Bone Marrow. I made a mistake."

"I know what you mean. Matt's been on this ward so often, I can see how you'd come back by habit."

Disoriented, David surveyed the rooms along the corridor. It seemed that Matthew had stayed in every one of them at various times. In the last six months (forty years ago?), this ward had become a second home.

In one room, he recognized (again as if through a haze) a ten-year-old girl bald from chemotherapy. When first diagnosed, she'd been riddled with tumors, but treatment had managed to cure her. Nonetheless, the patient's mother, unable to control her revulsion, had disowned her daughter, never once visiting, eventually divorcing her husband.

In another room, David saw an eight-year-old boy whose parents had considered his cancer an inconvenience to their routine. Every three weeks, on a Friday, they drove him to the front door of the hospital, let him out, and left while he found his way up to the Pediatrics Ward for chemotherapy. He stayed for the weekend, vomiting, the fear and loneliness in his eyes enough to make David want to strangle the parents, who drove back to the hospital on Monday and waited while a nurse brought the boy in a wheelchair down to the hospital entrance, where she helped him into the car.

But not us, David thought. Not us! Donna, Sarie, and I stayed with Matthew always, never letting him give up hope, never allowing him to feel lonely or succumb to despair. Taking shifts, and sometimes all three staying with him at once, they'd bolstered his spirits and let him know how much he was loved. They were his companions at all hours for his six months of treatment. Donna and David had probably seen Matt more than most parents saw their children, in snatches, an hour in the morning, an hour at night, for a lifetime.

Early in Matthew's treatment, a doctor had asked about David's work. "How's your fiction going? Any new books?"

Restraining his frustration, because the doctor was trying to be friendly, David had answered, "My work? Since Matt got sick, I've stopped writing. Right now, as long as it takes, my job is my son."

3

"Yes," David said to the nurse. "I made a mistake. I'd better get up to the Bone Marrow Ward."

"But you didn't answer my question. How's Matt doing? Is he okay?"

"The answer's too complicated. It depends."

"On . . . ?"

"If you look forward or back."

"What?"

"Right now, he's doing well."

"He's one of our favorite patients, you know. He's so brave. We love his sense of humor."

"So do I. Believe me, so do I. For what it's worth, I think you and the rest of the staff did a wonderful job."

"Keep us posted."

Yeah, David thought, but I hope the message isn't the disaster of my nightmare.

"I'll let you know. Right now I'd better get up to where I belong."

To the Bone Marrow Ward.

Toward what David was becoming more convinced was a desperate chance for salvation.

4

The Bone Marrow Ward. Logical, simple, ingenious, and if your case isn't in the right statistics, terrifying. You don't go there to be treated unless there's nowhere else to go.

Tumors are perversely fascinating in their capacity for evil. They may be the only organic substance that left unharmed and given nourishment lives forever. In laboratory conditions, they survive and survive. With

Matt, the initial combination of chemical agents (each combination is called a protocol) proved ineffective. After several administrations of it, a second protocol was tried, and that too proved ineffective. Matt's tumor became classified as resistant, an especially malignant life force. The third protocol showed results, however. The mass shrank 50 percent, and surgery (which would formerly have killed Matt, so large was the mass to start with) now became possible.

The surgeon explained that the operation would take eight hours. Matt would lose the diseased rib and maybe one rib to the top and bottom, depending on what the surgeon found. The principal risk was that the tumor had grown so close to the spine that in removing the tumor the surgeon might accidentally cut a nerve— or else the artery that supplies blood to the spinal cord— and Matt would be paralyzed.

"What are Matt's chances of that happening?" Fear made the question a whisper.

"Chances?" the surgeon had responded. "I do my best. I can't give odds. What happens to each patient happens to him one hundred percent."

So Matt, with utter calmness, allowed himself to be prepared for surgery. The nurse who took his heart-beat and blood pressure readings was astonished by how relaxed Matt's vital statistics made him seem. David, Donna, and Sarie walked beside Matt's bed as he was wheeled toward the surgical area. Then the family was told to go to a waiting room.

5

The waiting room. A horror in itself. Plenty of televisions and magazines, but everyone stares at the floor.

An eight-hour operation, and the major risk is paralysis, but the surgeon is optimistic and says he's going for total cure. So you know when three hours into the operation you get a message to meet with the surgeon, something's horribly wrong—and when not one surgeon but three of them join you in a consultation room, you know that whatever's wrong, it's worse than you can imagine.

"We ran into troubles," the first surgeon said.

"You don't mean he's paralyzed!" Donna said.

The second surgeon shook his head. "Not that at all."

"Then . . . ?"

The surgeons didn't respond.

"For God's sake, tell us."

"The tumor may be inoperable."

"*What?*"

"It metastasized," the third surgeon said. "It's not just on his rib."

Metastasized. When David later repeated that word to friends and business associates, he was amazed by how many didn't understand what *metastasized* meant. To spread. The tumor had sprouted seeds. Roots were growing throughout Matthew's lung.

"No!"

"The metastases are so close to the spine I don't think I can get them all," the first surgeon said. "I'll probably have to take several more ribs than I hoped." The surgeon exhaled. "And all of his lung."

David ached.

"The point is, if I don't get every offshoot from the tumor, several other tumors will start to grow, and in areas where I can't operate without killing him."

"He's going to die?"

The second surgeon nodded. "I'm sorry. You have to be prepared for that possibility."

"But isn't there *anything* we can do?"

The surgeons glanced at each other.

"The tumor's been resistant to chemotherapy," the third surgeon said. "The only thing I can think of is to *really* give it a dose, I mean a humongous dose, of chemicals. To go for a bone marrow transplant."

David vaguely recalled having heard the term before, but he had no idea what it meant.

"It'll take too long to explain right now," the second surgeon said. "The treatment's severe, much worse than the chemotherapy your son's already received. It's risky, but in many cases, especially leukemia patients, it's been known to work."

"But you've got to make a decision," the first surgeon said. "As soon as I opened Matt and saw what I was dealing with, I put him on hold. Don't worry about him for now. The respirator and the other machines are keeping him alive. But I can't leave him like that very long. You've got a decision to make."

What's the worst thing that ever happened to you? How about the worst question you ever faced?

"The options are this," the first surgeon said. "I can leave the tumor as it is. I can close Matt up. The tumor will continue to grow. But Matt will be able to have a more or less tolerable summer, provided he gets enough pain medication. He *will* be dead by the fall."

Donna's face streamed with tears.

"And the alternative?" David breathed.

"I can go ahead with the surgery, take several more ribs than I hoped, probably all of his lung, leave the parts of the tumor I can't get at, close him up, and hope that chemotherapy combined with a bone marrow transplant kills the rest."

"But remember, the tumor's especially resistant," the second surgeon said. "The bone marrow treatment might not work."

"And the treatment's extremely severe, worse than anything he's already been through. He could die from it," the third surgeon said. "He might not even have the tolerable summer he'd have if we took the first option and stopped the operation right now."

"I can't keep Matt on hold up there forever," the first surgeon said. "I've either got to stop the procedure or get on with it. *Soon.*"

"How soon are you talking about?"

"You've got fifteen minutes to make up your mind. And this is a one-time-only decision. You can't change your mind tomorrow or next week. Matt couldn't survive another exploratory operation of this scope. And if the tumor gets any bigger, I'd have to leave much more of it inside him, which means the bone marrow treatment would have a great deal less chance of being effective."

"Fifteen minutes?" David's voice rasped as if his throat were packed with broken glass. "If you just sew him up right now, he'll die for sure?"

"Sometime in the fall."

"And if you take out what you can and go for the bone marrow transplant . . . ?"

"He still might die, and you'd be denying him a tolerable summer. With the transplant, his summer would be a distress, to put it mildly."

Donna kept weeping. Sarie seemed about to faint. "Fifteen minutes?"

"Less than that now," the first surgeon said.

"And a one-time-only decision?"

"Correct."

"Tell me what to do!"

"I can't. That's why I came down here to speak with you. The situation's too complicated. It's up to *you* to make the choice."

"I can't"—David gasped for breath—"face Matt when he wakes up and tell him we did nothing. I couldn't bear the look in his eyes. I couldn't bear telling him that he doesn't have a chance—that he's going to die."

David looked for agreement from Donna and Sarie. Cheeks raw with tears, they nodded.

"Go ahead and cut the sucker out," David said. "Get as much as you can. We won't give up. Matthew's strong. He's proved it before. He'll prove it again."

"Just so we understand each other," the second surgeon said. "Whatever happens, it's extremely important to your mental health that you never second-guess this decision. You made it in good faith. Never reconsider it."

"Cut!" David said. "Get as much of that bastard tumor as you can!"

6

Another waiting room, this one outside Intensive Care. Matt's operation, as predicted, took eight hours. The chief of the surgical team came into the crowded room and found a place to sit across from David, Donna, and Sarie. His eyes were red with exhaustion. He was scheduled to perform another operation within an hour.

"How bad?" David asked.

There must have been forty people in the room, all afraid for their own friends or relatives. Eavesdropping unabashedly, they waited for the surgeon's answer. There are no secrets—privacy is impossible—in the waiting room for Intensive Care.

"Actually it went better than I expected." The surgeon rubbed his raw eyes.

David straightened.

"I only had to take four of his ribs and a third of his lung."

Only? When it comes to your son, and you were told he'd probably have a quarter of his body cut away, you actually feel a bizarre relief when you learn it was only a *fifth*.

"Then the roots of the tumor hadn't spread as far as ..."

"Not as extensively as I feared," the surgeon said.

"Then"—David took a breath, afraid to ask—"you actually got it all?"

The surgeon bit his lip. "No. There's a growth—it isn't big, the size of the tip of my little finger—that I had to leave against his spine. It wasn't just a matter of risking paralysis if I took it. I'd have killed him."

The other people waiting apprehensively to hear about their friends or relatives listened more intently.

"Oh . . ." David's voice dropped. He'd been warned not to hope, and yet he *had* hoped, and now he suffered the despairing consequences.

"As I told you, no matter how well the procedure went, I knew I wouldn't get what I wanted: total surgical cure."

"Then we go to bone marrow," David said.

7

Matthew was strong. David had promised the surgeons that, and the degree of Matt's strength was about to be proven. Matt's surgery had been so severe—"The most painful there is to recover from," the surgeon explained—that Matt had been scheduled for two days of intensive care instead of the usual one.

Nonetheless, twenty-four hours later, Matt's tortured body had so responded to postoperative treatment that he could be moved back to his room on the Pediatrics Ward.

"You were right. You son's constitution is remarkable," the surgeon said. Then turning to Matt, who was conscious though groggy from pain medication, he added, "But Matt, I'm afraid I'm going to have to keep being tough on you. I can't let you rest. I can't let fluids accumulate in your system. You're going to have to stand as soon as possible. You're going to have to make your bladder work."

Matt groaned. "Stand?"

"As soon as you're able. The important thing is you have to pee. I don't want to have to put a catheter back into your penis."

Matt groaned again.

The surgeon's pager made a beeping sound. From the small black box on his hip, a voice announced a telephone number for him to call.

"I'll be right back," the surgeon said.

Donna, Sarie, and a nurse followed the surgeon out, leaving David and Matthew alone.

David hesitated. "How are you doing, son?"

"I hurt."

"I bet."

Another pause.

"Well, let's get it over with," Matt murmured.

"What?"

"If I have to stand"—Matt groaned—"and pee, let's do it now so I can sleep."

God's honest truth. That's what he said. And don't be surprised that he could talk, much less be able to move. Maybe in the movies, patients are unconscious for days after serious surgery, while the actors have meaningful conversations at the bedside. But in real life, the physicians want you alert as soon as possible. In Intensive Care, Matt had been conscious enough and alert enough to write notes (his mouth had been blocked by a tube driving oxygen into his lungs) two hours out of surgery.

"The pain'll just keep on," Matt murmured. "He told me to stand. Let's do it. Help me."

Somehow, despite the oxygen prongs attached to Matt's nostrils . . . and the IV tube leading into his arm . . . and the tubes draining blood from an incision that curved from Matt's right shoulder blade down to his waist, then around his waist and up to his right nipple . . . somehow David and Matthew got Matthew out of bed.

Matt gingerly placed his bare feet on the floor. He gasped and wavered, while David held him up and at the same time held the IV stand.

David groped for a plastic urine bottle and supported it under Matt's penis.

David waited, it seemed forever.

Matt's knees began to buckle. David gripped his left shoulder more firmly.

"Hurry, Matt."

"I'm trying!" The force in Matt's voice must have been agonizing to him. "It doesn't want to come!"

"Then we'll try another time."

"No!" Matt almost sobbed. "I don't want another catheter! I don't want any more pain!"

Dribble.

The sound, so commonplace, made David's heart break.

Dribble.

David felt the warmth of the urine through the plastic bottle he held. That warmth was the most intimate sensation he'd ever known.

Dribble.

Thank God!

The dribbles stopped.

No!

Matthew's face contorted with strain. "That's it. Can't . . . make myself go anymore . . . tired . . . have to . . . get back in bed."

"Twenty-four hours out of major surgery and you're standing, peeing? You're the strongest, bravest person I've ever known. I'm proud of you."

"Have to get back in . . ."

"Bed? I know, son. Just a minute, and you can rest."

David set the urine bottle on the floor, eased Matt toward the bed, and that's when they discovered the huge mistake they'd made.

When Matthew's gurney had been wheeled down from Intensive Care, the nurses in the Pediatrics Ward had raised the bed in his room, gripped the sheet beneath him, and gently pulled him across from the gurney onto the bed. That bed, from which David had helped Matt to stand, had not yet been lowered. The mattress was as high as David's chest and Matthew's shoulders. Matt couldn't set his hips on the bed and lean back to rest.

Matt wavered, close to falling. David clutched Matt's left shoulder, released the IV stand, and reached for a button to summon a nurse.

But the button was too far away. David couldn't reach the button unless he let go of Matt. The IV stand started wobbling. David grabbed for it. Matt wavered so fiercely that David couldn't possibly expect him to try to edge toward the button that would summon a nurse.

The oxygen prongs fell out of Matt's nostrils. The tube that drained blood from Matt's huge incision stretched taught as Matt wobbled.

"Matt, I don't have the strength to hold your IV stand with one hand and use my other hand to lift you onto the bed."

"I can't stand any longer."

Why did I let myself listen to him? Twenty-four hours out of major surgery, and he's out of bed, clutching me, the two of us wavering like two drunks trying to dance. How could I have been so stupid?

"Dad, that chair."

"I don't understand."

"Can you reach the chair?"

"But *why?*"

"Do it." Matthew wheezed. "Pull it over here. I think if I can stand on it . . ."

That's when David knew he wasn't as smart as his son.

"Yes!"

David frantically released his hold on the IV stand. He grabbed the chair, jerked it toward him, and desperately regrabbed the IV stand just before it toppled, all the while using his left hand to hold up Matt.

"Do you really think you . . . ?"

"Just keep holding me, Dad."

Matt strained. Gasping, he raised a foot to the chair. David eased him up.

With a greater gasp, Matthew raised his other foot to the chair. David eased him higher.

Matt's hips were now level with the bed. He sat, clutched David's shoulders, and with the most terrible groan David had ever heard, lay back in bed.

David quickly reattached the oxygen prongs to Matthew's nostrils.

"So cold," Matthew said.

At that moment, as David pulled a sheet and blanket over his shivering son, the door to the room swung open. The surgeon stepped in, followed by Donna, Sarie, and a nurse.

"The call I had to return wasn't important," the surgeon said. "But your mother and sister and I had a good chance to talk. As I was saying, Matt, I hate to do this. Nonetheless, I need to keep being tough on you. As soon as you're able, in a day or so, you've got to get out of bed. More important, you've got to make your bladder work."

Through his pain, Matt grinned. "It's already taken care of."

"What?"

"Here," David said. He stooped and handed the surgeon the plastic bottle of urine.

The surgeon looked baffled. "But how did you . . . ?"

"Well"—David glanced with love toward Matthew—"you might say we went dancing. I think the bed could be a little lower."

"Wait a second. You don't mean . . . ?"

"You wanted him on his feet as soon as possible." David directed another loving glance toward Matthew, who kept grinning through his pain. "I promised you. My son's as tough as any patient you ever had."

8

Tough doesn't describe it. What do you say to a fifteen-year-old boy, who stood only five-feet tall and weighed only a hundred pounds and was totally hairless, whose cancer and chemotherapy had made his skin translucent . . . what do you say when he recovers from his mind-disorienting sedation after major surgery and realizes the extent of what's been done to him?

"Four ribs? A third of my lung?" Matt's eyes became panicked. His next question, though, so avoided the crucial issue that David's breath escaped him, pushed out by pity.

"Then I won't be able to play the guitar again?" Matt's voice broke. "I won't be able to keep up my—"

"Music?" David said. "The surgeon took some muscle tissue from your back and grafted in onto your chest where your ribs used to be. With some physical therapy, you ought to be able to have the strength to hold your guitar. Later, when you've stopped growing"—*if,* David thought, *if you get the chance to be old enough to stop growing*—"you'll have another operation, not as serious, to put a support brace into your chest, to replace the ribs you lost. You won't have a gap there. No deformity. You'll stand straight. As far as your lung's concerned, if you'd lost it completely, you wouldn't be able to breathe sufficiently to play on stage with a band. But you only lost a *third* of your lung. You won't run any hundred-yard dashes. You won't charge up a dozen flights of stairs. But you'll be able to walk as easily, with as little effort, as you did before. If you don't try to be Bruce

Springsteen and sprint around the stage, you still have a chance to be a musician."

"Still have a chance?" Matthew sensed the implication. He mustered the courage to ask the all-important question. "Still have a . . . ? How's my case doing?"

David, Donna, Sarie, and Matt's physicians had made a bargain with him from the day of his diagnosis. No one would ever lie to him.

"Dad? My case?"

"Not so good. The surgeon couldn't get it all." David held back tears.

Matthew knew that his tumor was resistant to chemotherapy, that only once had any combination of chemicals caused a response, and even then only a partial one. To the best of his information, surgery had been his final hope.

"Then I'm . . . going to die?" Matt asked the question as if he didn't understand the meaning of the words, as if they were gibberish or a foreign language. But all at once he did understand, and tears leaked from his eyes. "I'm going to *die?*"

A physician, who saw Matthew seldom and thus hadn't established rapport with him, responded. "You have to face up to it. There's a strong risk you might not survive."

At the time, David thought the doctor's response was so cruelly matter-of-fact that David wanted to grab the man, shake him, and curse him for his insensitivity.

But the physician, it turned out, had been forced to answer that ultimate question so many times in his career that he'd finally concluded that the only adequate response was to be direct and objective. An unemotional statement of the facts.

And the fact was that Matthew did have to be prepared. His chances of survival were narrowing. There *was* a likely possibility he would die.

"But"—Matthew sobbed—"I don't *want* to die."

"No one wants to die," the physician said. "Everyone eventually does, though."

"When they're old, when they've lived their lives."

"It doesn't always happen that way."

Matthew sobbed harder. "I'm just a kid."

No pain, no catastrophe that David had ever endured compared with the heartbreak Matthew's next sobbing statement caused.

"No one will remember me."

David wanted to scream.

Instead he held Matthew's hand and tried not to let him panic.

"If the worst does happen, I promise, son. You won't be alone. And you *will* be remembered. But no one's giving up. I told you, we've still got a chance." David looked with hope toward the physician. "A bone marrow transplant."

"Yes," the physician said. "Provided your son meets the requirements."

"Requirements?"

9

The start of another nightmare. During Matt's operation, when the surgeons had explained the unforeseen complications of his tumor, when a decision had to be made within fifteen minutes, there hadn't been time for the surgeons to discuss the conditions required for a bone marrow transplant.

There were four.

First, the bone marrow transplant unit wouldn't put Matthew through the extreme procedure unless there was a reasonable expectation that the treatment would succeed. To determine whether Matthew was a suitable candidate, the physicians had to know . . .

Second, whether the remnant of the tumor that the surgeon had been compelled to leave against Matt's spine was as small as the surgeon had described.

Third, whether the tumor was growing on any other parts of Matthew's body, on his legs and arms, for example, where Ewing's sarcoma customarily struck.

Fourth, whether his bone marrow was free of any microscopic evidence of tumor spores.

If any or all of these latter three conditions gave cause for pessimism, "all bets are off," the physician said.

Time was crucial. The sooner the answers were determined (provided they were encouraging), the sooner Matt could be given a bone marrow transplant. That quarter of an inch of tumor that for sure was still in his body, against his spine, would keep growing, and if it got much bigger, it might resist even the massive doses of chemotherapy with which the physicians would attempt to kill it.

Mentally, psychologically, emotionally, and physically, Matt had almost reached the limit of what a human being can suffer and withstand.

10

But the suffering persisted. Within forty-eight hours of Matt's surgery, he was wheeled from floor to floor, from ward to ward. Each bump made him cringe in pain. Each time he was transferred from his bed to various examination tables, he groaned and sweated. But he never screamed. He never panicked. He had chest X rays, skeletal X rays, CAT scans, magnetic resonance images. Some of these procedures required him to remain immobile, stifling his agony, for an hour.

Then his bone marrow had to be tested. Lying on his good side, fighting the excruciating stress on his bad side, he gripped David's hand with the force of a wrestler and endured the threaded point of a needle being screwed through each buttock and into each hip bone. The needle probed to the very center of each bone and extracted marrow.

David had no idea what marrow looked like. He imagined it resembled bone. But as the needle was unscrewed from each hip and its contents pushed onto a microscope slide, he saw that bone marrow looked like blood, the thickest, the darkest he'd ever seen.

The tests were completed. The waiting began.

Three days of unimaginably nerve-taut waiting while David, Donna, and Sarie worked every minute to make Matt as comfortable as possible and strained to alleviate his mental alarm.

"Hope, Matthew. Hope."

A sleepless son to a sleepless parent at three o'clock in the morning.

"Is there an afterlife?"

How does a father answer such a question from a son in danger of death?

David sat up from the cot beside Matthew's bed. He chose his words carefully, and each word tasted like salt. "Afterlife? I promised I'd never lie to you. The truth is, I don't know. There's no way to tell. I think there is. I want to believe there is. For sure, a lot of people *do* believe there is. But unless they get there, they'll never know."

"I'm pretty sure there's *something* after death," Matt said.

"You mean like heaven?"

"Sort of. I'm confused."

"We're all confused. So many theories. A lot of Eastern religions believe that we live many times and that when we die, we're reborn in a brand-new body."

"I've heard about that. What's it called? No, I remember. Reincarnation."

"I'm surprised you know that."

"I've been reading. I want more time. There's so much I want to learn about."

"You've learned quite a lot already."

"Not enough."

David forced himself to keep talking. "Those Eastern religions believe that eventually, after several lives, we die one last time and go to God."

"I remember. But . . ."

"What is it, son?"

"Am I *good* enough for God?"

That was one question David could answer without a doubt. "You're the finest person I know, the most honest, the most fair, the most decent. By all means, you're good enough, *more* than good enough for God."

"I love you, Dad."

"Matt, I can't express how much *I* love *you*."

12

The waiting finally ended. The results of the tests came back. Three physicians and a nurse surrounded Matthew on his bed, while David, Donna, and Sarie waited anxiously in the background. This was it. The day of judgment. And the physicians had such blank faces it was impossible to predict what they would report.

Hurry! For God's sake, tell us! David thought. With so many people crowding the room, he felt smothered.

"Matt, your bone marrow's clean. There's no sign of Ewing's sarcoma anywhere else in your body. The remnant of tumor on your spine is so small we can't see it on X rays. That and the fact that you recovered so strongly from your surgery makes us very much determined to go ahead with the transplant."

The room became silent. David couldn't believe he'd heard correctly.

But Matt showed no reaction.

"Matt, don't you understand? You've got a chance!" David kissed Matt's forehead.

A doctor started grinning. "And there's something else. The pathology results on the tumor showed it was necrotic."

"What?"

"Necrotic," another doctor said. "The tumor was partially dead. That's why it shrank after the investigational protocol."

"But then it started growing again," Sarie said.

"Because it got used to those chemicals. We've said all along the tumor's resistant to treatment. But the fact that some of it was dead proves it *can* respond. It's not completely resistant. Before, the tumor was huge, and the chemicals were given in non-life-threatening amounts. But now with such a small segment left inside and with the massive doses of chemicals we'll be giving you, we've got reason to hope we can kill it."

"Yeah." Matt started to grin.

13

But his suffering still continued. Another operation was required—to remove a pint of marrow from his hip bones, then to implant a tube in the right upper chamber of his heart (a match to the one that months ago had been inserted in his left chest) for the purpose of making it easier to administer the chemicals.

"In the long run, it's more painless," a physician said. "With the tubes in place, we won't have to keep sticking IVs into your veins."

David interrupted. "We understood that in January—when you put in the first tube. That first tube did its job well. But why this second tube? Why *so many* tubes?"

The doctor's answer seemed vague. "Well, sometimes a bone marrow transplant gets complicated." The doctor rubbed his neck. "Sometimes we need a few more ways to gain quick access to a patient's veins."

With so much good news, David didn't pause to consider this hint about possible disaster. His son had a chance. That was all he cared about.

14

Bone marrow is the substance within bones that produces blood. If a patient has a resistant disease (leukemia, for example) that attacks the marrow, the treatment consists of extremely high doses of chemotherapy, accompanied by full-body radiation. The effect of this treatment is, in theory, full destruction of the disease within the marrow.

Nonetheless, without healthy marrow to produce healthy blood, the patient will die. So healthy marrow has to be inserted into the body. This procedure is accomplished by, first, finding a donor (usually a brother or a sister) whose marrow is compatible with the patient's white blood cells. Marrow is then extracted from the donor and introduced into the patient. If everything works as it should, the donated marrow grows within the patient, produces healthy blood, and the patient is cured. Sometimes the patient's body rejects the marrow, and the patient is given marrow from yet another compatible donor. If the patient continues to reject donated marrow, there's no way to save that patient from the lethal effects of the massive chemotherapy. But more often than not, David learned, the treatment works.

The miraculous part of the procedure is that, while the marrow has to be extracted surgically from a donor, it's introduced into the patient's body through the simple means of pumping it through an IV tube. Because bone marrow, like a homing pigeon, somehow knows where to go. It enters a vein and flows toward its proper destination, the center of bones, where, marvel that it is, it feels at home and, God willing, multiplies.

A wonder of nature.

In Matthew's case, his marrow was not diseased, so he needed no other donor than himself. The pint of marrow that had been surgically extracted from him was combined with a chemical preservative, placed in a plastic bag, flattened in a metal tray, and frozen much below zero in a liquid nitrogen container that resembled a conventional freezer. The advantage of being a self-donor, of returning his own marrow to his own body, was that Matt didn't risk complications due to biological rejection of foreign marrow. What's more, since his cancer was localized, he didn't have to undergo full-body radiation as well as the chemotherapy. That was the good part.

But no matter if other-donated or self-donated, the marrow couldn't enter the body until the blood-destroying treatment was completed.

And that was the bad part. When you receive what

a physician calls "humongous" doses of chemotherapy, your blood becomes worthless. It has no platelets to enable it to clot if you're injured and start to bleed. It has no white blood cells to combat infection. It has no red cells to carry oxygen.

You get the idea.

Each day, for seven days, as Matthew received intravenous chemotherapy, monumental, life-threatening doses of it, a nurse wrote numbers on a chart on the wall. These numbers were in columns and referred to the various vital aspects of his blood.

And each day the numbers went lower. A white-blood count of six thousand is wonderful, but David, Donna, and Sarie watched Matthew's white-blood count descend to . . .

Zero.

That's when a simple ingenious system gets scary. Someone with a slight case of the flu can contaminate a bone-marrow-transplant patient, and instead of giving the patient a mild stomach upset, the flu makes him very sick indeed. Because the patient has no white blood cells to attack the usually mild infection. Further, the bone-marrow physicians can't assume that the patient's fever and nausea are merely produced by the flu; to guard against other, potentially lethal infections, they might be forced to administer unnecessary extreme medications.

Before entering Matt's room, David, Donna, and Sarie washed their hands thoroughly, then put on hospital gowns. They interrogated Matt's visitors to make sure no one had been exposed to even a cold. "Wash your hands. Put on that gown."

After seven excruciating days, and a day of rest that allowed the deadly chemicals to be purged from Matthew's body, his bone marrow was unfrozen and returned to him.

Cause for joy.

But Matt was fifteen, past puberty, though the hospital classified anyone under sixteen as a child. The preservative in his bone marrow, which worked well on children but caused occasional allergic reactions in adults, sent his blood pressure soaring to one hundred and seventy. His head ached so severely he told David he feared his skull would burst. He convulsed. His breath (because of a peculiarity of the preservative) filled his room with the smell of garlic, and that made him vomit. But medication reduced his blood pressure. The headaches and convulsions stopped. The garlic stench eventually went away. And everyone waited for a zero white-blood count to climb.

15

That was when David took his turn sleeping next to Matthew . . . when Donna went home to rest . . . when Donna returned to the hospital in the morning and David went home to run as was his custom . . . and stumbled into the house, couldn't stop sweating, filled a glass of water, raised it to his lips, and suddenly fainted on his kitchen floor.

16

Time present and time past
Are both perhaps present in time future,
And time future contained in time past.

—T. S. ELIOT
Four Quartets,
"Burnt Norton"

17

Floating.
His daughter grieving below him.
Hovering. His aged body succumbing beneath him.
Forty years later.
Or forty years earlier in a nightmare on his kitchen floor?
He didn't know! He didn't understand!
Rising. Drifting.
Floating through brilliance.
A radiant hallway. A splendrous door.
Pushing. The door swinging open.
Fireflies.
Power chords.
But where was Matthew? He had to save Matthew!

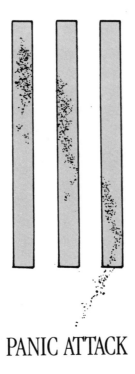

PANIC ATTACK

1

David struggled against his dizziness as he rushed from the Pediatrics Ward. The corridor, the rooms, the administration area, the blond nurse he'd spoken to—they unnerved him, as if he'd seen them only recently and yet remembered them from long ago.

My God, what's wrong with me?

The tingling that had started in his hands and feet had now spread up his arms and legs, rushing toward his heart.

He felt so off-balance he almost leaned against a wall. The humming behind his ears so disoriented him he wanted to sink to the floor. But he had to keep moving.

101

Hurry!

Matthew! He couldn't explain his fear that tomorrow afternoon his son would contract septic shock and eight days later die from its effects. Whatever had happened to him while he'd fainted, David *knew* what was going to occur. He could *see* it, as if each terrifying instant had been seared into his memory.

Lurching around a corner, he found an open door to an elevator and rushed inside. Vision blurry, he fumbled to press the button marked 7.

The doors hissed shut. The elevator surged upward. Again the pressure in David's skull swelled, making him grab his temples. He stifled the urge to vomit.

Abruptly the elevator stopped. Its doors opened. He staggered into a corridor, not sure which direction to choose (*but wasn't I here just this morning?*), then suddenly realized he had to turn right.

Down another corridor. A man and a woman stared at his unsteady movements. He fought not to waver.

Passing elevator F.

Passing elevator E.

Through a gradually clearing haze of memory, he regained his bearings.

Turn right!

He found a door, pushed through it, and hurried down still *another* corridor, this one lined with rooms in which elderly patients blinked listlessly at game shows on television.

"Now you've got to try to eat, Mr. Standish." A nurse raised a spoon of what looked like pea soup to the lips of an aged bone-thin man.

David hurried farther, passed a nurses' station,

pushed through another door, and at last he was here, at the source of his nightmare, the Bone Marrow Ward.

2

Its safety procedures were meticulous. Because of the danger of infection, the air inside this ward was filtered, purified, and recirculated every two hours. The nurses took off their gowns each time they left a patient's room and put on fresh gowns whenever they entered another patient's room. If a patient wanted to watch a videotape, the VCR was scrubbed with disinfectant before it was taken inside the patient's room. Every precaution (short of total isolation) was maintained.

And yet . . .

And yet . . .

David knew that tomorrow afternoon his son would . . .

He hurried toward the bin in which the fresh gowns were stored. Putting one on, tyings its strings, he noticed a worried mother carrying a tray of barely eaten food from her daughter's room. This woman (like the nurse in the Pediatrics Ward) he remembered vividly and yet as if from a great gap in time.

He tried to smile, though his dizziness made the ward seem to swirl, and managed to walk a straight line toward Matthew's room.

But when he peered through the open door, the bed was empty.

In David's nightmare, Matt had been helped down the hall and was having a bath right now. *If that turned out to be true, would everything else in the nightmare also come true?*

Panic rising, David turned . . .

And saw the most lovely vision he ever hoped to appreciate.

Not Matthew, though *he* would have been vision enough.

But Donna, who came around a corner, adjusting the ties on her hospital gown, and paused as David smiled at her.

David's smile was broad enough to hurt his cheeks, deep enough to squeeze his heart.

Donna, who had died in his nightmare at the age of seventy-nine, and who even then had seemed as beautiful as the day he had married her.

On his wedding day, he'd been so afraid to give up what he thought of as his freedom, even though he'd made the commitment to combine his destiny with hers, that he'd almost fled from the church.

But he'd abided by his commitment, and when he'd turned from the altar to witness his soon-to-be wife proceeding with such pride and dignity down the aisle, her white gown so magnificent, her brown eyes, auburn hair, and dark oval face so lovely, his heart had rejoiced.

Just as it rejoiced now as he stared at her with wonder—her experience-wearied features midway between the glowing smoothness he'd witnessed on his wedding day and the ashen wrinkles he'd seen on the day she died.

Despite the swirling in his brain, David walked toward her, put his hands on her shoulders, and kissed her tenderly on the lips. "I haven't seen you in a while."

She studied him with welcoming eyes. He swore they glowed. And he swore something else. As eerie as it seemed, he felt that *she* felt, she *knew,* that they were gazing at each other, with wonder, as if a miracle had occurred, from a perspective forward of another half-lifetime, of almost forty years.

"In case I haven't told you often enough," David said, "I love you."

Donna's grin was as winsome as when she'd been twenty-one or seventy-nine. And her humor was as endearing as ever.

"Oh, hell," she said and kept grinning. "Don't bore me."

"Deeply," David said. "Always. You don't know how much I mean 'always.'"

"Don't I? I *do* know. Yes!"

Inches away, they surveyed each other's eyes, and David was suddenly sure that he saw *behind* her eyes the same desperate knowledge *he* had, as if they had both returned, *both* been given a second chance. A reprieve. A miraculous opportunity. To reverse the greatest loss of their earthly existence.

To save their son's life.

"Yes, always," David said. "Deeply and forever, I love you."

Donna's grin changed to solemnness and, more, the epitome of determination. "I understand. Believe me, yes. Deeply. Forever. We've got a job to do, the greatest job of our lives."

David's festering question burst from him. "Where's Matt?"

"He went for a bath."

Just as in my nightmare! David thought.

"Dad."

Turning, David saw him.

3

The interval between extensive surgery and the bone-marrow transplant had permitted sufficient time for Matthew's hair to begin to grow again. Matthew's scalp was fuzzy with hair. He even had the shadow of a mustache.

But as Matt returned from his bath, holding his robe together with one hand while he gripped a portable radio in the other, he looked flushed. His eyes looked dull. And he was staggering.

"Jesus," David murmured.

He and Donna rushed to him. Matt wobbled, about to fall as they caught him.

"Almost lost my balance in the . . . almost cracked my head getting out of . . ."

"The tub," a nurse said behind him. "I kept a close watch. I held him tight, but . . ."

"Slipped. Dizzy," Matthew said. "Could hardly get out of the . . . nearly hit my head on the sink." He gasped. "Need oxygen. Can't breathe."

While the nurse took off her gown and put on a fresh one, David and Donna helped Matthew into his room. His knees kept buckling. They eased him onto his bed, then quickly used the sink in the room to wash their hands with disinfectant.

By then the nurse had joined them, washing her hands as well.

"Can't breathe," Matt repeated.

"What's wrong with him?" Donna asked.

David fought to control his dizziness.

"The effects of the chemotherapy. His low blood factors." The nurse's tone was reassuring. Nonetheless she frowned, checking Matthew's pulse.

"David, he's been like this since you left this morning," Donna said. "I'm worried—more than usual."

She had good reason to worry, David knew with inexplicable certainty. His arms and legs tingled in cold, then hot rushes.

"His heartbeat's slightly higher than normal for him. Eighty-five instead of seventy," the nurse said. "That's probably from the exertion of taking a bath and coming back to his room."

But her frown persisted as she wrapped a cuff around Matthew's arm and pumped it full of air to monitor his blood pressure.

"Need oxygen," Matthew repeated.

"Give it to him," David said.

"He probably doesn't need it. Most likely he's just short of breath from walking back to"—the nurse interrupted herself, putting a stethoscope to her ears, then watching a blood-pressure monitor on the wall behind the bed. "Slightly higher than normal for him."

Normal for Matt was one hundred and ten over seventy-five.

"What are the numbers?" David's voice was strained with urgency.

"One hundred and twenty over eighty. Well within an acceptable range."

"But *look* at him. He's sick."

"It's to be expected. After all the treatment he's had. When his blood counts start to rise, he'll feel a lot better."

"My stomach hurts," Matt said.

"As if you might vomit?" The nurse grabbed for a plastic basin.

"No." Matt gasped. "It burns."

"You might have ulcers from the chemotherapy," the nurse explained.

"But he's had six months of chemotherapy," Donna said, "and he never had ulcers before."

"Because he never had treatment in such large doses."

"Oxygen." Matt's chest heaved.

"Give it to him," David said.

"But I can't!"

"Why?"

"Here." The nurse handed David a sheet of paper. "Before he went for his bath, I took a sample of his blood—to have it analyzed for its oxygen content. The computer just printed out the results of the test. His blood gases are just what they should be. The lab test shows he doesn't need oxygen. If I give it to him, I'd hurt him more than help him. Oxygen's toxic to a patient's lungs if it's administered when he doesn't need it."

The tingling rushed from David's arms and legs toward his chest. His heart beat faster.

"But you said you took the blood-gas test *before* Matt went for his bath. Maybe he didn't need oxygen then, but what if his condition changed in the meantime? *What if he needs the oxygen now?*"

"His condition *couldn't* change that fast," the nurse said. "Not without something to indicate the change. I just took his temperature. It's normal."

David's lungs pumped. The swirling in his brain intensified. A peculiar kind of swirling. Not the sort in which the room seemed to spin. Instead the room remained still while his *mind* spun.

Again he saw fireflies. Again he floated down a brilliant corridor. Again he heard power chords.

But the fireflies could have been glinting specks behind his eyes.

And the power chords? David suddenly realized that Matthew's portable radio had been playing heavy-metal rock all along.

My God, is this really just a delusion?

And yet he *knew,* he was *sure* that Matthew's weakness and stomach pains were warnings of the septic shock that soon would kill him.

No!

He liked this nurse. She knew her job. She did it well. She was sympathetic, talented, motivated, and totally wrong.

I can't waste time. I can't let my son die.

His pulse thumped faster, increasing the humming behind his ears. He'd hoped to intervene subtly in Matthew's treatment, to point out this or that minimal change in Matt's condition, to maneuver Matt's physicians into humoring David's increasing concern and taking precautions that they saw no need for, given Matt's presently acceptable vital statistics.

But now he realized that if he did believe in his premonitions, he couldn't keep following the indirect tactic he'd chosen. He had to insist, to *do* and not just make suggestions, to act *against* the system instead of within it.

"Antibiotics," David told the nurse. "He needs them right now. Give them."

The nurse stepped backward. "What are you talking about?"

"Donna, do *you* understand?"

"Yes. Believe me."

Again David saw her in triplicate—as a vibrant bride in her early twenties, as a dying elderly woman, as the middle-aged desperate mother she was at present—all equally beautiful, each the object of the various lifelong, profoundly increasing stages of his love.

But at the moment, he thought he'd never loved her more. And *again* he was struck by something behind her eyes, a frightened conviction, a terrified certainty, as if she truly *did* understand what he was warning about.

"Antibiotics. Matt needs them. Give them to him. *Now,*" David told the nurse.

"But I told you"—the nurse stepped farther back—"he doesn't have a temperature. His other statistics are somewhat high but well within normal ranges. There's no *reason* to give him antibiotics. Even if he had an infection, which he doesn't, we'd need to do lab cultures on his blood, to learn what kind of infection it was, so we could decide what kind of antibiotics would be best to fight the—"

"Who's the doctor on duty?"

The nurse veered quickly past David, her eyes no longer nervous but apprehensive. "I'll hurry and get him."

"No, I'll go with you. Donna, in the next ten minutes, Matt'll be so weak he won't take phone calls. He'll send away visitors, the friends he's been anxious to hear from. He'll ask you to turn off his music. Understand? He'll start rejecting everything that's important to him."

"Yes," Donna said, that same unsettling knowledge behind her eyes. "I understand. Do it. Whatever you think is right. I'm so afraid."

"Twice is too many times."

Donna nodded, as if she sensed exactly what he meant.

With a frightened look, the nurse left the room.

David followed.

4

In the corridor, the nurse whispered to the head physician, her remarks attracting a second physician. They turned, eyes narrowed, as David approached.

The first physician straightened. "We gather you're having some reservations about your son's treatment."

"Fears."

"That's understandable." The second physician cleared his throat, obviously hoping to avoid an awkward conversation in public.

"You're following the procedure you explained to me. I understood the logic of that treatment. I agreed," David said.

"Well, good," the first physician said. "Then we don't have a problem."

"No," David said. "Everything's changed now."

"Changed? Because he feels weak? But we told you that would happen."

David's heart kept pounding. "Yes, but something else is going to happen. All the early symptoms are there, but you don't know it yet . . . because you're not expecting it, so you're not"—his lungs heaved—"you're not interpreting the symptoms—"

"I beg your pardon?" The second physician narrowed his eyes. "I'm not interpreting . . . ?"

"The symptoms the way you would if you knew what was going to happen."

"Going to happen?" The first physician frowned at his colleague.

The parents of other patients had begun to gather and listen.

"Can we go somewhere else to have this talk?" the second physician said.

"As long as we get this settled."

"There's a conference room down the hall."

5

They shut the door to the narrow room that had a blackboard upon which doctors customarily drew diagrams for parents confused about the treatment their child would receive. Both physicians studied David as if they wished they weren't alone with him.

"Now we realize you're under stress," the first physician said. "You're worried about your son. All perfectly natural. But what exactly do you think's—?"

"Going to happen?" David's legs felt weak. He gripped a chair. "Septic shock."

The second physician narrowed his eyes. "Where'd you hear that term? Something you read? You've been doing, let's call it, well-intended but uninformed research, and it makes you nervous?"

"Never mind how I know. I'm absolutely certain—"

"Now listen carefully," the first physician said. "Whatever books you've been reading, whatever outdated texts have made you afraid, yes, it's true there's always a danger of septic shock. We've already warned you. When a patient's blood counts are low, there's a risk of infection. That's why we take extreme precautions to prevent—"

"No, *you* listen carefully." Though the room stayed perfectly still, David's mind revolved. "Your precautions are fine. There's nothing wrong with the treatment you're giving him. But Matthew *will* get septic shock. I can't explain why, but tomorrow afternoon, he'll become infected. His blood pressure will drop and . . ."

"What makes you so sure?"

"You wouldn't believe me! Just give him antibiotics *now!*"

The first physician edged toward the phone.

The second physician raised his hands in a placating gesture. " 'Antibiotics' is a general description of a wide variety of treatment."

"I understand that. Different antibiotics have applications to different infections."

The first physician picked up the phone.

David's chest felt squeezed. "Stop. Give me a chance."

The first physician touched numbers on the phone.

"Please!"

The first physician hesitated.

"You need to know the specific infection so you can choose the specific antibiotic to use to attack it. So now I'm telling you."

As David spoke the words that to anyone but a doctor would have been gibberish . . . as he recalled the words he'd memorized from the microbiology report in his dream . . . words that in his present timestream would have been impossible for him to know, let alone pronounce . . . he realized that he *wasn't* crazy. His dying vision was fact. He had indeed come back.

For what he told the physicians, the words like gravel in his mouth, was . . .

"What'll give Matthew septic shock? *Streptococcus mitis. Staphylococcus epidermidis.*"

David couldn't believe he'd spewed those chunks out.

The physicians couldn't believe it either.

"Where the hell did you . . . ?" The first physician almost dropped the phone.

The second physician drew his head back. "But naturally adapted strep and staph are almost never . . ."

"Fatal?" David shuddered. "This time they will be."

His legs buckled. The room spun along with his brain. He lost his grip on the chair.

"My God, he's . . ."

Falling.

"Having a . . ."

Drifting.

Toppling.

"Heart attack."

6

When David struck the floor, he couldn't move; he felt disoriented, helpless. His fall, which seemed to have lasted forever, contrasted sickeningly with the sense he had of floating above his aged dying body. He seemed to drop and rise simultaneously—conflicting sensations that produced such vertigo he could barely muster the strength to blink.

Making these reactions more intense was the added element of fear, as if to move, to try to stand, would kill him.

Through a haze, he saw the first physician lunge from the room. The second physician knelt beside David, checking his pulse. After an interval—ten seconds? a minute?—the first physician rushed back, accompanied by Donna and a nurse.

"His pulse is strong." The first physician's voice was an echo. "No fibrillation. Ninety."

"Acceptable," the second physician said.

"No . . . normal for me is . . ." David's chest heaved.

"Don't try to talk."

The nurse wrapped a blood-pressure cuff around David's arm. Donna knelt beside him, touching his cheek, as the nurse inflated the cuff. David saw the fear in Donna's eyes.

The nurse deflated the cuff, watching a dial as she listened to a stethoscope pressed to David's arm. "A hundred and forty over ninety."

"Tolerable. A little high, but not unusual. Not critical," the second physician said.

"No. Listen. Normal for me is . . ."

"Don't try to talk. Relax."

Sure, easy for *you* to say, David thought, the room and his mind aswirl.

"What I told you a minute ago might not be true. Try not to worry. Our initial examination isn't conclusive, but you might not be having a heart attack."

"Then *what* . . . ?"

"We don't know. We've alerted Emergency. We're sending you down there. If it *is* a heart attack, we're not equipped to deal with—"

"Stop the spinning. *Stop the damned room from spinning.*"

"David, I'm here. I'll be with you," Donna said. "I'll stay right beside you."

116

"No, stay with *Matthew*." The effort to emphasize his words was excruciating.

David felt his body being lifted. He suddenly found himself in a wheelchair. He closed his eyes. But the tingling—and worse, the swirling—persisted.

Feeling the wheelchair being pushed, he groaned from increasing dizziness. Pressure accumulated behind his ears. He dared to open his eyes and discovered . . .

He was in an elevator. The doors hissed shut. The elevator dropped.

"No!"

At last he moved of his own accord, shoving his hands to his ears to stifle the pressure.

"No!"

The elevator jerked to a stop. The top of his head seemed about to explode. If someone hadn't been holding him, he'd have toppled from the wheelchair.

Blinding lights. A swirling corridor.

But not the soothing gleam of the corridor in his nightmare. This was the hospital's first floor. Rear section. The part that patients and visitors almost never saw and prayed they would never *have* to see. Through a spinning maze of twists and turns, he was rushed in his wheelchair toward the Emergency Ward. Outside, a wailing ambulance arrived. David concentrated to focus on glass doors that led to a curve in a driveway where attendants unloaded a patient onto a gurney. Through a blur, he saw a nurses' station directly across from where the glass doors now slid open, the attendants hurrying the patient through.

David's wheelchair stopped abruptly in front of the nurses' station. His head tilted forward, making him groan.

A woman peered over a computer screen toward him. "Name?" She poised her fingers above a keyboard.

David managed to tell her.

"Two 'r's, two 'l's?"

David gasped for breath and nodded.

The woman tapped the keyboard. "Address?"

"It's all"—David sweated, even though his skin felt cold—"on file. I hurt my shoulder . . . in March." He breathed faster. "I came here then for treatment. I'm in . . . the computer file."

"Just a minute." The woman tapped the keyboard again. She read an address from the screen. "That's where you live?"

David nodded.

The woman read the name of an insurance company.

"Yes," David breathed.

"Okay, you can take him in."

The wheelchair hurried forward. David's dizziness increased. He closed his eyes once more, felt the wheelchair turn sharply left, and the next time he looked, he was speeding toward an examination room—a bed, a sink, a metal cabinet, its shelves stacked with medical supplies.

The nurse who had wheeled him down from the Bone Marrow Ward stopped and tapped his shoulder. "They'll take care of you now, Mr. Morrell. Good luck. I've got to get back on duty upstairs."

At once, another nurse replaced her. "Can you stand?"

"Don't know."

"Try. I have to get you onto the table."

She gripped his arms and helped him to his feet. Wobbling, he leaned his hips against the table and settled backward. She raised a metal bar on each side of the table to keep him from rolling off.

A male resident came in, closing a curtain.

"Pulse is ninety," the nurse said.

"Not critical."

"No, listen to me." David felt as if a ten-pound rock had been set on his chest. "I tried to explain upstairs." He squirmed from the humming pain behind his ears. "I'm a runner. My heart rate's low. It's normally sixty."

"Blood pressure—one hundred and forty over ninety."

The resident shrugged as if to say "not critical" again.

"You don't understand." David shivered. "It should be a hundred and fifteen over seventy-five. It's *never* . . . God, that curtain."

The resident frowned and turned toward the privacy curtain. "What's wrong with—?"

The curtain was decorated with blue wavy lines. David's mind not only spun now but wavered in imitation of those lines. Sickened, he closed his eyes again but still saw the wavy lines. His breath was so rapid he felt he'd just run several miles. The top of his head seemed to bulge.

"I'm going to . . ."

Faint?

Die?

Toppling toward his kitchen floor.

Floating toward the radiant doorway.

Fireflies gleaming.

(Behind his eyes?)

Power chords throbbing.

(In his head?)

Then?

Now?

Later?

"What's *happening* to me?"

"That's what we want to find out."

The nurse unbuttoned David's shirt. The resident pressed pads against David's chest. Squinting, David saw that the pads were attached to wires that led to an EKG machine on a cart.

The resident flipped a switch on the EKG. Needles wavered, making inky marks on paper.

The paper rolled from the machine. The resident tore off a sheet and studied it.

"Yes, I found the problem. Here. And another one. *Here.* And *here.* Extra blips. Your heart. There's something wrong with—"

"Let me see it," David gasped.

"What?"

"Let me see it."

David reached for the printout. The effort to focus his eyes was agonizing. "No, that's . . . not what's wrong with me."

"What are you talking about?"

"Those blips . . . normal for me."

"Normal?"

"My EKG . . ."

"Relax."

"Always looks like this."

The resident frowned. "Have you had medical training?"

"No."

"In that case . . ."

"But I've always had a"—David grabbed the sides of the table as it started swirling—"right . . ."

"I don't understand."

"Right . . . bundle." David struggled to complete his statement. "Right bundle branch block."

The nurse and the resident stared at each other.

"Right bundle branch block?" The resident seemed astonished, as if he'd never expected a patient to speak to him in technical medical phrases.

In contrast with David's certainty about the septic shock that would soon kill his son—*have to save him!*—there was nothing mysterious about his present medical knowledge. The phenomenon in his heart had been explained to him years before. The heart is a pump, and like any other pump, it needs an energy source, "electricity" produced by the body. Nerves, like wires, control the flow of energy, and under normal circumstances, this energy flows smoothly from chamber to chamber, stimulating the heart to take in and push out blood.

But in David's case, a cluster of nerves, a "bundle branch," on the right side of his heart had deteriorated. Energy impulses, which usually flowed in an orderly fashion, had been interrupted and forced to redirect themselves along another branch of nerves, taking longer to reach the right side of his heart. On a printout from an EKG machine, this redirection of energy produced an extra blip within an otherwise normal heart wave pattern.

The blip was not alarming, as long as you knew what it meant, and David's condition wasn't considered lethal. For twenty years, he'd run an average of four miles every day, and even though he was foolishly a smoker, he could finish that run and never be out of breath. So whatever was wrong with him, he was sure that the bundle branch block hadn't caused it.

But something *was* wrong. Without a doubt. Pausing often to gasp for air, he described his symptoms.

Tingling.

Shivering.

Sweating.

Rapid heartbeat.

Rapid breathing.

Pressure on his chest.

Humming behind his ears.

Swelling in his head.

And swirling.

Terrible swirling.

David thought, If *you* had these symptoms, what would *you* guess was going wrong? A heart attack? You bet that's what you'd guess. No, never mind guess. We're talking fear.

"Okay, the extra blips match what you're telling me," the resident said. "A right bundle branch block."

"Then what"—David's chest heaved, both his lungs and heart—"is wrong with . . . ?"

"We'll do more tests. Hang on. We're trying, Mr. Morrell. We'll do everything we can to find out."

The nurse inspected David's right arm. "His central

vein's good and thick." She stuck an intravenous needle into the vein and extracted blood.

David felt too disoriented to feel the prick of the needle.

"Get lab tests as soon as possible," the resident said.

The nurse rushed away.

7

And just then Sarie walked in.

Beautiful wonderful Sarie.

As when David had seen—too weak a word—*witnessed* Donna in the Bone Marrow Ward (after three hours of having been away or else half a lifetime), David's soul swelled with love. Again, as when he'd seen Donna upstairs, he had the eerie sense of a triple image: of Sarie as a smooth-faced infant, of the glowing twenty-one-year-old she now was, of the haggard woman who wept beside his deathbed.

I'm going crazy, David thought. That's what's wrong. I'm not sick. I'm nuts.

And yet . . .

And yet . . .

Why am I so sure of *when* and *how* Matt'll die?

Sarie's blue-eyed, blond glow of young adulthood was dimmed with shock. "I just got out of class. I went up to visit Matt. Mom told me . . ."

"Yeah." Despite his rushing heart, David did his

best to grin. "Mom told you . . . I've got a few problems."

Sarie clutched his hand. "She said you wanted her
to stay with Matt, so I came down to see . . ."

"I'm glad you did." The pressure in his head swelled,
making him grimace. "It's good to have you with me."

Someone brushed past the curtain, entering the
room. A woman. Not a nurse. She didn't wear a gown
but slacks and a blazer. ". . . neurologist," she finished
explaining. "I understand you collapsed an hour ago."

An hour ago? David would have sworn he'd been
in the Emergency Ward for less than ten minutes.

"What are your symptoms?" the neurologist asked.

For a second time, David described them. Tin-
gling . . . rapid . . . pressure . . . swelling . . . dizzy . . .
humming . . .

The resident enumerated David's vital statistics.

The neurologist frowned. "They're not consistent
with a heart attack.

David turned to Sarie. "Matt?"

"He can hardly move. His girlfriend called. He
didn't have the strength to talk to her."

It's starting, David thought. The infection's building. I'm seven floors below him. I can barely move, but
I'm the only one who can save him.

"Grip my hands," the neurologist said.

"What?"

"Grip my hands."

David obeyed.

"Squeeze them as hard as you can."

David squeezed until her fingertips turned white.

"Good." The neurologist took off his shoes and

124

socks, then pressed the blunt end of a pen down the balls of his feet.

His toes curled inward.

"Good." She tapped a rubber hammer against his elbows, knees, and ankles. His reflexes jerked.

"Good."

"Stop the damned room from spinning."

The resident checked David's pulse. "What the—? It's up to a hundred and ten."

The neurologist straightened. "Blood pressure."

"Up. A hundred and fifty over ninety-five."

"Sarie, go back upstairs," David blurted. "Go back to Donna. Tell her, whatever happens to me, tell her—"

"Mr. Morrell, has anything happened to you in the last few days? To change your medical—"

"I fainted this morning."

"Fainted?"

"I went out running. I came back, started to drink a glass of water, and . . . "

"You ran in this heat and *fainted?*" the resident said. "You're probably dehydrated."

"No! I drank plenty of water after I woke up!"

"Electrolytes," the neurologist said. "They must be off-balance."

"No!" David said.

He understood about electrolytes. They were elements in a person's blood that allowed the body's "electricity" to flow efficiently through vital organs. But if these elements weren't present, the "electricity" couldn't flow, and the vital organs went into shock. The principal electrolytes were potassium and sodium.

"No!" David repeated. "I swallowed a potassium pill. I put salt on my palm and licked it."

"Have you had *medical* training?"

"Sarie, get back to Donna and Matt!"

"His pulse is up again," the resident said. "A hundred and fifty."

"Pressure," the neurologist said.

"A hundred and sixty over—"

David felt such swelling in his chest and head, such heaving in his lungs that—

"I'm going to die," he said.

"Code blue?" the resident asked.

Despite his delirium, David recognized the hospital's signal for summoning maximum help in case of imminent death.

"Code blue? Should I call it in?" the resident repeated.

The neurologist opened her mouth, her lips forming "yes."

"Wait, his pulse is coming down," the resident said. "A hundred and forty."

The neurologist rubbed her forehead. "Pressure?"

"Down. A hundred and fifty. Code blue?"

"Not yet."

"His pulse is down again," the resident said. "A hundred and thirty."

"Pressure?"

"Down. A hundred and forty."

The room became silent. In David's swirling mind, the walls seemed to narrow.

"His pulse is down to a hundred," the resident said. "His pressure's a hundred and thirty."

David's delirium began to clear. He stared at the cabinet to his right and managed to steady his vision.

"Pulse?"

"Ninety."

"The same as when he came in here. Pressure?"

"A hundred and twenty. Almost what he says is normal for him." The resident shook his head. "This thing's like a roller coaster, suddenly up, then down."

The neurologist rubbed the back of her neck. "I don't know. Labyrinthitis maybe." She referred to an infection of the inner ear that affected a person's ability to balance, making the patient dizzy.

"No," the neurologist corrected herself, "that wouldn't explain the pressure on his chest. Mr. Morrell, apart from your fainting spell after running this morning, has anything else happened to change your medical condition?"

"The last six months have been the same."

"I don't understand." She responded to a sudden thought. "When did you eat last?"

"This morning. Or maybe last night. I don't remember."

"You don't *remember?*"

"There isn't always time. It's been mostly hospital food, and . . ."

"Hospital food?"

"*Dad*"—Sarie clutched David's arm—"*tell* them."

"Tell us what?"

"About *Matthew,*" Sarie said.

"Who's . . . ?"

"My son." Despite his dizziness, David told them everything.

In hesitating gasps.

All of it.

A breathless babble.

The turmoil of the last six months.

Every fear-filled instant.

"Mr. Morrell," the neurologist said, "you've just had a panic attack.

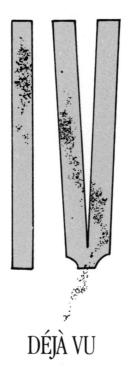

DÉJÀ VU

1

"Of course, I feel panicked! Didn't you listen! My son has cancer! Six months of chemotherapy! I watched him lose his hair! I held him while he vomited!"

"Take it easy," the resident said.

"I watched him get weaker, watched him stagger, watched him get thinner! They tried every goddamned chemical they thought would work! He lost four ribs . . . a third of his lung! He had a bone marrow transplant! Three weeks ago, I didn't even know what a bone marrow transplant was! They . . . !"

"Try to relax," the neurologist said.

"If I don't do something, Matt's going to die!"

The nurse who'd rushed off with samples of David's

blood pulled open the curtain, entering the room. "His tests came back."

The neurologist reached for the computer printout and scanned it. The resident peered over her shoulder.

"Look at those numbers," the resident said, amazed.

"You found it?" David asked. "You know what's wrong with—"

"These numbers indicate you've got—"

The neurologist interrupted. "The healthiest blood I've seen tested this year. Cholesterol—one hundred and seventy-nine. Well below the danger level. Creatinine—point nine."

David had never heard of creatinine. He was sure the term was unfamiliar to him. And yet . . .

He recalled his seizure on the kitchen floor this morning. A shudder aggravated his tingling.

Creatinine, he understood suddenly, was an element in blood that indicated how well a patient's kidneys were functioning. The lower the number, the more efficiently the kidneys were filtering poisons from the body.

How do I know this? David thought.

His 0.9 was excellent, David realized, as if he'd been taught it many years before. An average person had a creatinine level between 0.1 and 1.1. Over 1.1 meant the kidneys weren't working as hard as they should. Over 3.0 meant the kidneys were failing. Over 4.0 meant the kidneys weren't working at all. Unless emergency procedures were taken, the body's toxins would accumulate to a fatal level.

In David's nightmare on his kitchen floor—or in his memory, floating over his deathbed—when Matthew had contracted septic shock, one of the major consequences had been kidney damage. The kidneys had shut down totally (though temporarily, David had been told). Matthew's urine had stopped completely. He'd been put on dialysis to vent excess fluid and filter toxins from his blood. But despite the dialysis, Matthew's creatinine had risen to—dear God!—the lethal level of 4.5.

And even *that* hadn't been what killed him!

2

Had?

Would?

But none of these disasters had happened! They were only from David's nightmare! And yet he knew, tomorrow afternoon Matt's unexpected septic shock would set them in motion!

Have to get up there! Have to save . . . !

The neurologist kept reading the results of David's blood tests. "Sodium, potassium, chloride . . . electrolytes all normal. No sugar problem. Mr. Morrell, I repeat, you've had a panic attack."

She raised her hands. "Yes, I understand you're worried about your son. You're afraid for him. But that's not the kind of fear I'm talking about."

Sarie spoke quickly, "What do you mean?"

The neurologist continued to stare at David. "For the past six months, you've been in a constant state of increasing crisis. Each stage of your son's treatment has been more prolonged and more extreme."

"Extreme? Every time the damned phone rings . . ."

"You jump? Your knees get weak? Of course. You're afraid you'll hear more unnerving news about your son's condition, a worse diagnosis of . . ."

"His pain, his horrible pain. I don't know how he bears it. We tell him he's been through the worst, and then something else goes wrong, and he needs some other kind of treatment, and the worst turns out to be nothing compared to . . . ! I don't know how he keeps up his strength! How can he be so brave? He never complains! He . . . !"

The pressure behind David's eyes broke. Tears streamed down his face. "Matt's just a kid! How can he be so strong?"

"You're proving my point," the neurologist said. "After six months of constant chaos, your body finally told you it reached its limit. Imagine if you'd almost been in a traffic accident. A truck veers toward you, forcing your car off the road. You manage to stop an instant before you hit a tree. What's your reaction? Your stomach feels on fire. Your heart races. You can't catch your breath. In effect, you've been having that near-accident for the past six months. I could give you a lot of technical words about neurotransmitters in your arteries and the *nucleus locus ceruleus* in your brain, but basically what it comes down to is, your crisis glands have been working constantly, to the maximum. And you've become used to it. You think it's normal, because for the last six months, it's all you've known. You're so saturated with adrenaline your body can't deal with the chemical effects any longer. You're hyperventilating, and that makes your heart pump faster, and that makes you dizzy. Of course the dizziness makes you more afraid. That in turn makes you hyperventilate more extremely, and that in turn makes your heart pound faster and . . . you're trapped in a terrifying, worsening, self-perpetuating circle. The more your crisis glands pump, the more they *will* pump because they're reinforced by fear. A panic attack. And if the cycle isn't stopped, the ultimate consequence is total physical collapse and possible catatonia."

The neurologist paused. "One more thing. In a panic attack, the patient usually feels tingling only in his hands, but *you* described tingling in your feet as well, and that makes this one of the most extreme examples of a panic attack I've ever diagnosed. You need rest. A lot of it. *Now.*"

"But my son . . ."

"Is under constant professional care. In the four hours you've been down here . . ."

What? David thought, pulse rising. *Four hours?* It seemed as if he'd been in the Emergency Ward for only forty-five minutes.

"In the four hours you've been down here," the neurologist continued, "I've asked for several reports on your son's condition. His physicians tell me he's doing fine. He's weak, but that's to be expected, given what he's been through. The main thing is, he's stable, and his treatment seems to be effective."

"No! He's going to die!"

"Should I call for help?" the resident asked.

The neurologist studied David.

135

"Maybe we ought to sedate him," the resident added.

"No," David said. "No, please, don't sedate me. Don't put me to sleep. My son . . ."

The neurologist scribbled on a prescription pad. "But sleep's exactly what you need. Your daughter can have this filled at the hospital pharmacy. I'm prescribing Valium for you."

"*Valium?*"

"Whatever you've heard about the drug, don't let the name shock you," the neurologist said. "Don't give yourself another attack. These pills won't knock you out. But they will make you groggy. You'll feel like taking a nap. You'll wake up calmer, rested. After your daughter gets this prescription filled, I want her to take you home and put you to bed. *And to make sure you take the medication.*"

"But my son . . . !"

"Two days from now, you'll adjust to the medication. You'll feel a little slow perhaps, but much less excited, and you'll be able to function. By then, you can come back and visit your son, as long as you don't try to drive. In the meantime, your wife will be with your son. The doctors will supervise him constantly. He's in good hands. There's nothing to worry about."

Two days from now? David thought.

Two days from now?

But that'll be too late!

3

The glass doors hissed open. A nurse pushed David in a wheelchair from the Emergency Ward. Beneath a concrete canopy, in a curve of the driveway where hours earlier David had seen attendants unloading a patient from an ambulance, Sarie was waiting in her yellow Fiesta.

The nurse stopped the wheelchair, opened the Fiesta's passenger door, and eased David inside.

His every movement remained an effort. His vision continued to swirl. Nonetheless he noticed Sarie move a small white paper bag—a pharmacist's green bill was stapled to it—off the passenger seat so he could get in.

The nurse shut the door. "Get some rest now, Mr. Morrell." She added to Sarie, "Make sure he takes those pills. Put him to bed as soon as he gets home."

"Don't worry," Sarie said. "I guarantee my Dad'll be a model patient."

Sarie put the Fiesta in gear, then steered around the curved driveway, heading toward the Emergency Ward's parking lot. The pivot of the car made David's mind reel. He wanted to clutch his skull, but given what he planned to do, he didn't dare alarm his daughter.

She turned right, onto a road that passed several university dormitories and a recreation building. Students thronged the sidewalks. The warm June sun was low in the sky, casting shadows. David raised his watch, squinting at its hands. Seven-thirty in the evening, and as near as he could tell, he'd entered the Emergency Ward shortly after two o'clock.

He couldn't understand how the time had passed so quickly.

Time! He didn't have much time!

"I'm sorry I took so long coming back," Sarie said. "The hospital pharmacy closes at six, but I managed to get them to stay open long enough to fill the prescription. Then I wanted to go back upstairs and see Matt."

"I hope you didn't tell him what happened to me." When David had collapsed, he'd been in a conference room with two doctors. In theory, Matthew didn't know about the panic attack.

"No. Mom didn't tell him either."

"Good. I wouldn't want to upset him."

"But I took Mom aside and told her what the neurologist said was wrong with you. Mom's worried. She says you have to take care of yourself."

David nodded, the effort painful.

"Mom says she can stay with Matthew. I'm supposed to ask a neighbor to bring up a change of clothes for her. When we get a chance, Mom and I will trade places. She'll come home and see if you're okay."

"Oh, I'm okay," David said with effort. "You heard the neurologist. I'm in perfect physical shape." He stifled the bitterness in his voice. "Except I'm terrified."

"But Matthew's doing fine."

"No! He going to—!"

Stop! David thought. You can't alarm her! You need her help!

"Matt's going to what?" Sarie asked.

"He's sicker than he's ever been before."

"But that's because the chemotherapy this time was stronger than he's ever received."

David pressed her hand. "Of course. He's bound

to be sicker this time. Forgive me. I'm just a little confused."

Fireflies.

Power chords.

4

Sarie turned right again (more swirling in David's head), proceeding down a main road toward an intersection, where if they turned left they'd be heading home.

But if they turned *right*, they'd go back to the hospital, not to the Emergency entrance in the rear but to one of the entrances along the front that David always used when he went up to stay with Matthew.

"Sarie, don't ask questions. Turn right."

"But . . ."

"Don't ask questions, I said. I know it's the wrong direction. It'll take us back to the hospital. *Just turn right.*"

"But I'm supposed to . . . What about the pills you were ordered to . . . ?"

"I'll swallow them. I promise. I've got something I have to do first. If it works, I promise I'll take the pills. I'll go to bed."

"But what do you want to do?"

"I can't explain it now. Just do what I say. Listen to me. I'm begging. Turn to the right."

Sarie stared at him. "You're sure you know what you're doing?"

"So sure you can't imagine."

Devotion made her acquiesce. "Okay, Dad. I don't want to get you more upset, but I don't want to be irresponsible."

"Trust me."

"Didn't you tell me never to trust anyone who says that?"

"This is different."

"Why?"

"Because I'm your father."

Sarie had almost passed through the intersection. "And I'm your puzzled daughter. I hope I'm not making a mistake. Trust you? Okay, then, Dad, hang on. Here we go." She jerked the steering wheel toward the right (David's skull came close to exploding) and drove down the lane that would take them to . . .

5

The ramp, where David had parked early in the afternoon. Now the family had three cars at the hospital: David's Porsche, Donna's Voyager, and Sarie's Fiesta. The gang's all here, David thought bleakly.

"Dad, that neurologist is going to be pissed at me."

"But I'm going to love you more. That's a wonderful trade-off, don't you think? And believe me, no matter if you think I'm going crazy, just keep trusting

140

me. I've never been more sure of anything. I know I'm right."

David staggered from the Fiesta, Sarie holding him up as he wavered from the parking ramp. Strangers frowned at them.

"But what are we doing?" Sarie asked. "Where are we *going?* Tell me. *Explain.*"

"I can't. You wouldn't believe me. It's too complicated. But maybe forty years from now we'll talk about it."

"Forty years from now? You're scaring me, Dad."

"With a lot of help from you"—or God, or I don't know what, David thought—"we're going to save Matt."

Sarie frowned.

Again David went through the entrance he always used. Again he went down the corridor that early this afternoon had seemed so familiar and yet so distant in time. With Sarie holding his arm, he did his best to keep from wavering, to keep from attracting attention.

They reached the large mirrored room that contained the chairs and the grand piano. Sarie guided him toward elevator E.

"No." David recalled the terrible pressure he'd felt descending the elevator toward the Emergency Ward. "I can't take elevators anymore. We have to use the stairs."

Sarie opened a door beside the elevator.

David's footsteps echoed as he staggered into a stairwell. He peered up toward seemingly neverending stairs that made him think of a mountain.

"Keep holding my arm. Maybe, just maybe, I'll manage this." He gripped the railing. They started up.

At each landing, David wanted to sit and rest, but breathless, he fought harder upward.

"Dad, you'll make yourself sicker."

"I don't matter."

"You're not making sense."

"Keep holding me."

The higher David climbed, the weaker his legs felt. He had a sudden recollection of his nightmare about his death forty years from now and a thought he'd had of life being like a steep flight of stairs that got harder and harder to climb as he got older.

That memory from his nightmare made him stop in distress. Everything he'd done since waking on his kitchen floor had been motivated by his frantic conviction that the nightmare was more than just a fainting spell. The scenes from his nightmare depicting how his life would be for the next forty years had been so vivid, so real that he'd believed in them.

But now he realized that in none of those nightmarish memories had he suffered a panic attack the day before Matt contracted septic shock. In none of those memories had he been rushed to the Emergency Ward. In none of them had he and Sarie struggled up these stairs.

Was his nightmare really only that? Just a nightmare, the consequence of nothing more than a fainting spell? Were his premonitions about Matthew only the consequence of a vivid dream and too much tension for too damned long?

"What is it, Dad? You stopped. What's wrong? Do you need to sit down?"

"I just thought of something."

Maybe the neurologist was right. Maybe I should go home. Maybe I'm being hysterical.

Fireflies.

Power chords.

Wavering on the stairwell, he seemed to float above his deathbed and drift through a brilliant doorway.

No! It's too real!

With tingling certainty, he understood now why the panic attack and the Emergency Ward hadn't been in his nightmarish memory, why he couldn't recall Sarie helping him stagger up these stairs.

Because they'd never happened. Forty years from now, how could he remember what had never occurred?

What he *did* remember was that after he regained consciousness on the kitchen floor, he'd been so shaky, so disoriented he'd been forced to stay in bed till tomorrow afternoon; and when he'd finally felt steady enough to return to the hospital, Matthew had contracted septic shock.

That day in bed was what had happened in his memory. Not any of the events of this afternoon and this evening. But now the neurologist wanted David to spend the next two days away from Matt.

No! I've been given a second chance!

An *alternative* to the past. Somehow, for God knows what reason, I've been allowed the chance to come back and *change* the past.

The more he thought about it, the more irrational the notion became, and yet he'd never felt saner in his life. Faith. He had to *believe*. Because if he did go home and spend the next two days in bed, if Matthew did die from septic shock, in that case David would *certainly* go insane.

"Dad, are you sure you're okay?" Sarie looked pale. "You're shaking."

"I just needed to rest for a second. Come on. We've got a job to do."

David struggled higher. They reached the third level. Sarie started to guide him upward toward the fourth.

"No," David said. "We're here. Open this door."

"But the Bone Marrow Ward's on the *seventh* floor."

"We're *not* going to the Bone Marrow Ward."

"Then where *are* we going? There's only one place I remember going to on the third floor."

6

The Pediatrics Ward, where Matthew had received his conventional and then investigational chemotherapy, where David had mistakenly gone instead of to the Bone Marrow Ward at the start of the afternoon.

The blond nurse was still on duty, evidently working a double shift. "You're back again." She looked surprised. "Has something happened? Have you got good news about Matt?"

"Doctor . . ." David gave a name, the physician they'd first met when Matt was diagnosed. "Is he on the ward?" The effort to ask the question increased his dizziness.

"I know he makes his rounds this time of the evening. Is he"—David's heart raced, the start of another panic attack—"is he here?"

The nurse frowned at Sarie supporting her father. "He was. I'm not sure if he went home."

"Please," David breathed, "find out."

"Sit down over here," the nurse said.

"No, I'm not sure I'd have the strength to stand again. Just find him. *Get him.*" David leaned against a wall.

The nurse left quickly.

"Dad, you ought to be at home."

"Matt's all that matters. *We have to save him.*"

"But he's not in any danger."

"Danger? You don't have the faintest notion. It's a second chance. We can . . . !"

"Yes?" The physician David had been hoping to find was suddenly before him. "What do you mean, Mr. Morrell? Save Matt? Second chance?"

"Thank God, you're still here."

"One of my patients had a complication. Otherwise I'd have been home for dinner now. What's wrong? You're out of breath."

"Three questions."

The physician looked tired. But because he'd diagnosed Matthew and seen him more than any other doctor, he had a special interest, indeed a special relationship with Matthew. This physician, more than any other David had encountered, had sacrificed his medical objectivity, had allowed his compassion to surface and to threaten his peace of mind.

145

"Three questions." The physician leaned next to David against the wall. "Okay, why not?"

"Suppose you knew that Matt, tomorrow afternoon, at four-thirty-six—"

"What are you saying? How can you be so specific?"

"Let me finish. Suppose you knew that precisely at that time Matt would contract septic shock?"

"That's the first question? I hate to hear the next one."

"And the septic shock would be caused by *streptococcus mitis* and *staphylococcus epidermidis?*"

"Where did you learn those terms?" The physician studied David's anxious gaze and sighed. "Okay, strep in his body and staph on his skin. Normal bacteria we always have in and on our bodies, and our bodies normally keep them in check."

"Except Matt's got a zero white-blood count, so he can't combat them."

"You've asked your second question. What's the third?"

"How would you stop the septic shock from happening?"

The physician stared at David. "You're serious?"

"Do I look like I'm kidding?"

"The obvious answer is antibiotics."

"Then do it. Go upstairs and give Matt antibiotics."

"This is all hypothetical."

"Please!"

"Even if it *wasn't* hypothetical, the Bone Marrow Ward isn't my department. I don't have authority there."

"Then go up and ask someone who does have the authority to do it."

146

"You really *are* serious?"

David trembled.

"Have you got some reason to be worried? Has Matt got a fever?"

"Not the last time I heard." The pressure behind David's ears increased. "But he *will* have. At three o'clock tomorrow afternoon. And they'll give him antibiotics then. But it won't be soon enough. Ninety minutes later he'll go into shock."

The physician pushed himself from the wall. "I don't understand why you're so sure he'll go into shock. The way you look, this entire conversation, I'm quite concerned about you."

Sarie couldn't stop herself. "Dad, tell him you just got out of the Emergency Ward."

"What?"

"My Dad had a panic attack. He's supposed to go home, stay in bed, take Valium, and . . ."

"Sarie, keep out of this."

"Is your daughter telling the truth?"

David nodded.

"Then go home and do what you've been told."

"I'm begging you to humor me. Why can't Matt have the antibiotics *now?*"

"Because we don't give antibiotics unless a patient has symptoms. At the very least, a fever."

"But suppose you knew Matt *would* get a fever, and after he got the antibiotics, they wouldn't have time to work before the shock set in and killed him?"

"We don't know anything of the sort. You're upset—that's obvious. So I'm trying to set your mind at ease, but—"

"What's wrong with giving the antibiotics ahead of time, *just in case?*"

"What's wrong with that?" the physician asked, an edge of impatience in his voice. "Because antibiotics are toxic to the body and could make your son sicker than he already is. That's one. And two, if antibiotics *are* given before an infection starts, the bacteria get used to them, so if an infection does start, the antibiotics are less effective. Now, please, Mr. Morrell, it's late. I've tried to be cooperative, but I've been here since six o'clock this morning."

"My son's going to die! Why won't anybody listen to me?"

The nurses in the ward stared in David's direction. Sarie looked distraught.

The physician cleared his throat. His tone became more authoritative. At the same time, it was strained with a greater effort toward tolerance. "For what this is worth, if it helps any, I've been monitoring your son's progress in the Bone Marrow Ward. Everything's proceeding on schedule. And if an infection does develop, the antibiotics have already been ordered from the hospital's pharmacy. They're in his room, ready to be administered. Of course, we can never be sure what infection might develop, but the types of broad-spectrum antibiotics they've got ready for Matt are especially effective against strep and staph. In that respect at least, you've got nothing to worry about."

David struggled to keep from sinking. Breathing deeply between bursts of words, he forced himself to say, "Unless the strep and staph have already started multiplying, and by the time his fever starts, his infection will already be out of control." He straightened, trying to prove he was functional, ignoring the pounding in his chest. "If Matthew did die from septic shock, by hindsight would you think the only way to prevent his death would have been to give the antibiotics ahead of time—before his fever started?"

"It's all hypothetical!"

"But what I just described to you . . . giving the antibiotics ahead of time . . . that's the only other way he could have been saved?"

"Could have? We can't predict the future. We deal with facts."

David had learned what he wanted. "My daughter's right. I ought to be at home. To take my pills and go to bed."

Sarie relaxed.

"I apologize for getting upset," David said, suddenly anxious to leave.

"No need. What pills were prescribed?" the physician asked.

"Valium."

"In a few days, you'll feel better, more at ease."

"I certainly hope so. In fact, I'm convinced of it."

"Come on, Dad." Sarie tugged his arm.

"I confess I feel worn out," David said.

"Well, after six months of what your son and you and your family have been through, of course you feel worn out," the physician said.

"But Matthew more than all of us. Come on, Sarie. I guess I've been a pain in the ass. It's just that I feel so helpless."

"Cancer's a roller coaster," the doctor said. "Up

and down, then up and down. Exhausting. Nerve-wrack-
ing. At the moment, your son's doing fine. Now it's your
job to take care of yourself."

"I intend to. Thanks again."

David wavered, escorted by Sarie.

"Wait a minute," the doctor said. "I'm finished for
the evening. I'll walk down to the parking ramp with
you."

No! David thought. Don't come down with us! If
you do, I'll have to—! He glanced at the blurred hands
of his watch. Almost 9:00 P.M. Time. He was—*Matt*
was—running out of time.

7

In the parking ramp, the doctor walked with Sarie and
David toward the Fiesta. The doctor waited till they got
inside before he moved toward his own car, almost as
if he'd been making sure that David would indeed go
home.

David glanced back toward the hospital. No, I have
to get up to the Bone Marrow Ward! As Sarie drove
from the ramp, he felt trapped, but he knew he'd never
be able to convince her to stop and let him out of the
car.

The sun was setting; shadows thickened.

Sarie parked in the gravel driveway of David's house.
She helped him inside, took him upstairs, made him lie
in bed, then brought him a glass of water and one of

150

the Valium. David put the pill in his mouth and raised the glass of water to his lips.

"I feel a little hungry," David said.

"What would you like?" Sarie responded eagerly.

"Maybe a sandwich."

"Tuna?"

"Fine."

Sarie hurried toward the kitchen.

David ate the sandwich, drank a glass of milk, and went to sleep.

Or pretended to, because he'd never swallowed the pill. Instead he'd tucked it along a cheek, and when Sarie went to the kitchen, he'd removed the pill and hidden it.

He lay in the murky bedroom, kept his eyes closed when Sarie came in to check on him, and struggled to control the swirling in his mind.

Can't go to sleep.

Mustn't let myself.

Don't dare to.

He heard dim voices, indistinct music, the television set downstairs. He glanced at the glowing numbers of the digital clock on the bedroom bureau. Ten-fifty-five.

Sarie, get tired! Go to bed!

Waiting was agony. Groggy, he felt himself drifting.

Hovering?

No! He concentrated on Matthew, on his son's scarred shrinking body, on the septic shock that would start at four-thirty-six tomorrow afternoon.

At midnight, he said a prayer of relief, hearing Sarie

151

turn off the television. She came upstairs, tiptoed into his bedroom to check on him again, then went to her own room.

He heard her door snick shut.

At 1:00 A.M., he took his chance. Off-balance, he staggered from bed, managed to dress, and peered from his room down the hallway toward Sarie's door. No light gleamed beneath it. He crept in the opposite direction down the shadowy hallway. Carpeted stairs muffled his footsteps. He slowly unbolted the front door, inched it open, stepped into the dark, and eased the door shut.

8

The night was unusually warm for June, heavy with humidity. Streetlights glistened off dew in the grass. Except for a distant car, the only sound David heard was the screech of crickets.

Sarie's Fiesta was parked beneath her window in the driveway. He couldn't risk using his spare key to start it, for fear of waking her. He had no choice. He had to walk. Under normal circumstances, the ten blocks to the hospital would have been effortless, an easy jog for a man with a twenty-year habit of running four miles each day. But at the moment, those ten blocks might as well have been ten miles through knee-deep snow.

Nonetheless he had to do it.

Get started, he told himself. You lazy bastard.

He stumbled across the lawn, across the street, and

past the grade school his son had attended. Despite the swirling in his brain, his thoughts were lucid. At least, he hoped so.

Staggering the way I am, a police car might stop me, he thought. I look like I'm drunk or on drugs. I have to use sidestreets, the darker the better.

So what should have been ten blocks turned out to be farther as he took a zigzag route from one murky street to the next. He felt lonely, helpless, and desperate, but terribly determined. His chest heaved from the pounding of his heart.

At last, he saw a glow in the sky. Not the morning sun. Even with his plodding gait, it was far too early for sunrise. No, what he saw was the gleam, reflected off clouds, of the sprawling complex of the hospital. Here, streetlights were unavoidable. He paused beneath a lamppost to study the blur of his watch.

Twenty minutes to three. Normally, he could run a mile in nine minutes, and now it had taken him an hour and forty minutes just to walk it. On the verge of collapse, he leaned against the chain-link fence of a university tennis court and studied the hospital, narrowing his vision toward the seventh floor of a brightly lit section to his right. The Bone Marrow Ward. Matthew. And if his nightmare was correct, a second chance.

For salvation.

To reverse the greatest loss of his life.

Suddenly bolstered, he released his grip on the fence and walked stolidly forward.

Matthew.

Fireflies.

Power chords. He marched to their rhythm.

9

He studied the parking ramp. Few cars. Insects swarmed around arc lights surrounding the hospital. No one was in the area.

David's six months of coming and going here had taught him how deserted the hospital could be at night, with the patients asleep, their visitors gone home, and the staff reduced. It was possible to walk down corridor after corridor and never see anyone.

That happened now. Inside the complex, the grand-piano room was deserted. Smothered by silence, David considered taking elevator E, but the pressure behind his eyes warned him not to. He opened the stairwell door beside the elevator. Continuing to respond to the rhythm of the power chords, he proceeded step after relentless step up the stairwell, no longer needing his daughter's support. Driven by his nightmare, he climbed higher. Third floor. Fourth floor. The numbers were fuzzy, but he kept climbing. Sixth floor.

Seventh floor.

10

At last he stopped and took a deep breath. Had to. From exhaustion. He wanted to slump on the stairs. And sleep.

How much he wanted to sleep!

Not yet. Time enough for sleep when his duty had been completed. Forty years from now. Tonight.

He opened the stairwell door and entered a corridor. Ten paces farther, turning right, he proceeded toward the Bone Marrow Ward.

Passing through one door, then along a corridor and through a second door, he entered it.

Softly. Silently. Seeing no one.

In most wards, a nurses' station would have been the first thing a visitor saw. But in the Bone Marrow Ward, the nurses' station was out of view, around the corner to the left. That corner was ten feet farther ahead than the corner to the right. And Matthew's room was just around the nearer right corner.

That made it possible—

David had calculated, had *depended* on this—

made it possible—

if a nurse didn't happen to prowl—

for him to shift unseen around that right corner and ease into Matthew's room.

It was after 3:00 A.M. Often at this hour, Matthew woke from nightmares and needed to talk to whichever parent was sleeping in the room with him, to express his fears and ease his apprehensions. Some of David's most intimate and heartbreaking conversations with Matt had occurred at this time of night.

But this afternoon, when David had last seen his son, Matt had been so weak it was doubtful he'd waken from his stupor tonight. David had depended on that as well. So much depended on faith.

The room was dark. Matt lay motionless in bed. Donna slept on a cot in the corner, breathing restlessly, enduring her own nightmares.

David shut the door till only a crack allowed light

to enter from the outside corridor. Responding to habit, he almost went to the sink to wash his hands, but he froze, realizing he couldn't make a sound.

When his eyes adjusted to the dark, he stepped toward Matthew's bed. Two IV stands supported bottles from which a dark liquid (probably platelet concentrate to give Matt's impaired blood the ability to clot) and a clear colorless liquid (probably saline solution to keep him from dehydrating) were pumped through tubes into IV connections implanted in his chest. Beside the bed was a cart upon which full syringes lay in a row: medications that Matt would need in case of an emergency.

David took the syringes one by one to the light that came through the crack in the door and studied their labels. Though he knew he shouldn't have been able to recognize their arcane names and understand the effect of each drug, he could do so now, and that made him more convinced that he was right, that his nightmare was more than just a fainting spell.

The first syringe he examined was labeled "carbenicillin." The term, so close to "penicillin," obviously named an antibiotic, but intuition controlled him, for somehow he knew it wasn't the particular antibiotic that Matthew needed.

He examined another syringe. Gentamicin. That too was an antibiotic, he realized, but again he had the certain knowledge that it wouldn't be effective against strep and staph.

Vancomycin. *He'd found it.* Though why he was sure, he didn't know, except for the memory of his nightmare.

Instead of a needle, the syringe had a blunt point

capped with a rubber stopper. He removed the stopper, held the syringe upright, and squeezed its plunger until liquid trickled out, guarding against an air bubble entering Matthew's system.

He stepped toward Matthew.

And stiffened, heart pounding, as a shadow blocked the crack of light at the door.

A nurse! It must have been time for her to make rounds, to check on the patients assigned to her, to administer whatever medications were scheduled.

Donna sighed, as if waking up.

David's chest heaved, panic swelling.

Hide! I've got to—!

The nurse spoke softly to someone else in the corridor. The shadow moved from the crack in the doorway.

David hurried. Despite the absence of a needle on the syringe, he knew he'd have no problem injecting the antibiotic. Too often, he'd watched the nurses add medications to his son's IVs. The tubes leading into Matthew's chest had access vents. All David had to do was unplug a vent, insert the blunt end of the syringe into the port, and squeeze the syringe's plunger—slowly, struggling to control his shaking hands—until all the liquid had entered the tube and drained toward Matthew's chest.

Twenty seconds later, his task was accomplished. For better or for worse, he'd done what he believed in his soul was the reason he was here after forty years. His thought was irrational, he admitted. But so was faith. His lingering doubt no longer mattered. He'd done everything in his power to save his son.

He shoved the empty syringe into his pocket, peered

down at Matthew, wanted to kiss his forehead, but stopped the impulse for fear of waking him. The resultant conversation would wake up Donna, and the further conversation would surely attract the nurse, whose shadow again blocked the crack of light at the doorway. David leaned against the sink, his heartbeat thunderous.

Better to confront than be confronted, he thought.

He opened the door, held his breath to control his hyperventilation, and stepped from the room.

The nurse was surprised. Before she could speak, David closed the door behind him.

"Mr. Morrell," she whispered. "I didn't know you were up here."

David took several steps along the corridor, gesturing for her to follow, guiding her away from the door. She hadn't been on duty when he'd collapsed this afternoon. He hoped she hadn't been told.

"I couldn't sleep," he said. "So I figured I'd come over to the hospital and look in on Matt."

"He's resting comfortably."

"I noticed. When I saw him this afternoon, he said he felt sick and weak. I was worried."

"He still feels sick." The nurse seemed puzzled. "But the thing is, he doesn't have a fever."

He *will* have, David thought. Tomorrow, at 3:00 P.M.

"We've been giving him Maalox to help settle his stomach."

"Good."

But Maalox won't stop him from getting septic shock, David thought. I pray to God the Vancomycin will.

"I heard you weren't feeling so well yourself when you came to see him this afternoon," the nurse said.

David shrugged, an embarrassed grin. "I got a little wobbly. Too much strain, I guess."

"It's understandable. This has been a long ordeal. But as soon as Matt's blood counts start to rise, it'll all be over."

It might be over sooner than you expect, David thought, if the Vancomycin doesn't work.

"I guess I'd better get going. I'll see you tomorrow," he said.

The corridor seemed to tilt. He needed all his strength to stay upright.

"Try to rest," she said.

"Believe me, now I will."

Because there's nothing more I can do, he thought, and somehow he walked steadily along the corridor, passing through a door.

A minute later, he reached the stairwell beside the elevator, only to realize he didn't have the strength to descend the stairs and walk back home. He staggered along a deserted corridor, found a plastic-covered sofa, and slumped on it.

Even with his eyes closed, he saw wavering lights. He clutched his stomach, hoping he wouldn't vomit. The sofa spun. At once, the wavering lights exploded into a million gleaming specks. He hovered in a radiant doorway, seeing fireflies.

And sank.

11

"You son of a bitch . . . !" Hands shook him. "You meddling . . . !"

David was pushed and shoved awake.

"You've been up here so long you think you've got a doctor's degree? A license to practice medicine?"

David squinted toward sunlight glaring through a corridor window.

"What?"

"Maybe you'll try surgery next?"

David rubbed his beard stubble and managed to focus on the physician he'd spoken to last night on the Pediatrics Ward.

The physician was livid. "I tried to humor you. I did my best to treat your hysteria with respect. And what do you do? How do you repay my patience? You come up here in the middle of the night and decide you're a candidate for the Nobel Prize in medicine! Look at *this!*"

David saw the blur of an empty syringe.

"I found this in your pocket! When the nurse on duty realized the Vancomycin was gone, she phoned her supervisor. The staff looked everywhere! Then your daughter woke up and discovered you weren't at home. She phoned your son's room. Your wife's so upset she might have a panic attack of her own. And here I find you sleeping with the damned empty syringe in your pocket!"

"What else could I do? I had to save him."

"Save him? You might have killed him! I told you

antibiotics are toxic if they don't have an infection to fight!"

David jerked upright. *"Matt's worse?"*

"No! No thanks to you! But *Doctor* Morrell, since that's who you seem to think you are, now that you've given him the Vancomycin, you've forced us to keep giving it at regular intervals. Otherwise an infection might not respond if we wait till Matt possibly does get a fever and *then* start giving the antibiotic. You've forced us into a preventive procedure we hadn't planned to try!"

David sank back onto the couch and exhaled wearily. "I didn't have a choice."

"You had a choice. To let us do our job. Practicing medicine without a license. Do you know how serious that is? Do you have any idea how much trouble you're in? You might end up in jail."

"Do you think I care? If what I did saves my son, *do you think I care if I do time?* That's what I'm trying to buy! For Matt! Time!"

"Well, buddy, if he dies because of what you did . . ."

David surged to his feet. *"If he dies, how much worse can I be punished?"*

Startled, the doctor stepped back.

"How late is it?" David asked.

"Almost noon."

"Give me till three o'clock. No, make it later. Till four-thirty-six."

"What difference does—?"

"If Matt doesn't have a fever by three and septic shock by four-thirty-six—"

"How can you be so specific?"

161

"Then call the cops, press charges, and put me away."

"Never mind three o'clock. I'm about to pick up the phone right now."

"But if I'm right, if the fever hits at three and Matt's blood pressure drops at four-thirty-six—"

"How can you be so specific?"

"Then forget the cops and hope I saved Matt's life."

"I'll ask you one more time."

"How can I be so specific? Because I've suffered through it *before!* I know what's going to happen. And if it doesn't, thank God I'm wrong. But I'm *not* wrong. And everything I described *is* going to happen. Matt died once. I won't let it happen again."

"My God, you're crazy."

David wavered. "Just give me till four-thirty-six. After that, do anything you want against me."

"But don't you see the flaw in your logic? If Matt was about to develop an infection, since you gave him the Vancomycin the infection won't occur. He won't have a fever. He won't go into shock."

David shook his head. "Without the antibiotic, the infection would have hit him like a fire storm. But believe me, don't ask how I know this, call it a nightmare, the infection will still be strong. I'm praying the drug I gave him will keep the bacteria from raging out of control."

"I've never heard anything like this."

"I've never *experienced* anything like this. You think I didn't realize I could go to jail if I gave him the Vancomycin?"

162

"You're that sure of what you did?"

"I could have given him the Gentamicin and carbenicillin, too. But I knew they wouldn't work on the staph and strep that'll cause Matt's infection."

"How in God's name did you know they wouldn't work against staph and strep? You've been spending all your time reading medical texts?"

"No. I can't explain it. I just knew. There's one way to prove it, isn't there? Wait till three o'clock—when Matt's fever's going to start."

The doctor looked startled by David's certainty. "I'm appalled by the risk you took. Disgusted by your irresponsibility." He shook his head. "Why on earth am I starting to . . . ? Don't test my patience anymore. Get lost. I don't want to see you till three o'clock. But listen carefully. If what you're so sure about doesn't happen, it'll be my pleasure to testify against you."

"Fair enough."

"*More* than fair. If I didn't like Matt so much . . ."

"That's the point, though, isn't it? Matt. He *has* to be saved."

"*And you don't think we've been trying?*"

"You and everyone else, you've acted perfectly. What you don't understand is, something you never expected is about to happen."

"What *you* don't understand is, till three o'clock I want you out of my sight so I can pretend I didn't find this syringe."

"You don't know how much I thank you."

"Thanks? What you need now are prayers."

"I'm praying, too, believe me."

David staggered toward an exit.

12

David's impulse was to rest in the rear of Donna's mini-van in the parking ramp. But he feared he'd fall asleep and fail to wake up before three. He also worried that if the authorities started searching for him, a logical place to look would be his wife's car. So he spent the interval pacing through the parking lot at the university's football stadium two blocks away, pausing often to lean against cars and bolster his strength. He'd expected the hours to drag, but they passed with astonishing speed.

He returned to the Bone Marrow Ward five minutes before three. A crowd had gathered—the physician in charge of the ward, several associates and nurses, the doctor he'd argued with at noon, and Sarie and Donna. The medical personnel frowned as he approached.

David held his head up.

The physician in charge of the ward stepped forward. He kept his voice low to avoid disturbing the parents of the other patients. But his whisper might as well have been a shout. "What I'd like to do to you, you don't want to hear."

"In your place, I'd feel the same. Please, you've got to trust me."

"Got to? The only thing I've got to do"—the doctor glared at his watch—"is phone the hospital attorney in a couple of minutes. We checked your son's temperature just before you arrived. It's perfectly normal."

"It's not three o'clock yet."

"One minute to," the doctor said.

"Then I guess it's almost time you checked his temperature again."

"My pleasure. So I can pick up that phone." The physician spun and entered Matthew's room.

David took two more steps, stopped before Sarie, and hugged her. "I'm sorry I tricked you."

"Dad, I . . ." Tears trickled down her cheeks. "Why did . . . ?"

"The simplest reason I can give, is I *had* to." He turned to Donna. "Sweetheart, I know you must think I'm . . ."

Donna touched his arm. David felt as if a spark leaped through him. Her eyes had a depth that he'd never seen in them, except yesterday afternoon when he'd hugged her, after what felt like years instead of hours. Again he had the dismaying sense that she truly understood.

But how was that possible? If *she'd* come back, why hadn't *she* given Matt the antibiotic? Doubt surged through him.

"Okay, it's three o'clock," the physician from the Pediatrics Ward said. "It's time to prove I wasn't a fool to listen to you."

"Let's go."

13

They entered Matt's room.

Matt's flaccid pallid face was appalling. It took enormous effort for him to whisper, "Dad, what's going on?"

"Don't be afraid."

"But they say you gave me . . ."

"All you have to know is I love you."

The nurse slipped a plastic sleeve onto a metal tube. The tube was attached to a box that showed digital temperature readings. She slipped the sleeved tube into Matthew's mouth. David sensed the anger and skepticism around him.

The box was timed to beep in three minutes.

The silence lengthened. The red numbers on the box kept changing, starting at zero and climbing toward . . .

The timer beeped.

"Absolutely normal," a physician said, his tone a mixture of relief and indignation.

Normal? David thought. Matt *should* have started a temperature!

The doctor in charge of the ward braced his shoulders. "I've got a phone call to make."

The physician from the Pediatrics Ward shook his head at David. "Looks like you're not the medical expert you thought you were." He didn't add what David guessed he was thinking—And I was foolish to think you might impossibly be right.

"For what it's worth," David said, "you can't know how glad I am to be wrong."

"Dad, wrong about what?"

"My imagination got the better of me. Don't worry. At least, no harm was done. You're safe."

"No harm?" the doctor in charge of the ward said. "Your imagination might have jeopardized his treat-

ment. Your amateur medical practice is about to put you in—"

"Just wait a few more minutes." David's momentary doubt was suddenly replaced by a certainty that made him quiver.

"Wait for what? You've had all the time you deserve."

"I just thought of something. If the antibiotics I gave him started to work, if they started to subdue the staph and strep—"

"Which we have absolutely no reason to assume will—"

"Matt's temperature wouldn't start to rise when I expected."

"It won't rise at all!"

"You don't understand how strong the infection was."

"*Was?* You mean how strong you think the infection *might* be."

"*Will* be. The schedule's been delayed," David said. "Give me fifteen minutes more. Just to put me at ease before—"

"You've had all the leeway you'll get!"

"I just took his temperature again," a nurse said.

The doctor stared toward the numbers on the box.

"His temperature's up."

14

The ensuing events were so rapid the doctor didn't have time to call the authorities. He and his staff were too busy working.

"My stomach," Matt said. "It feels worse. I'm going to—"

Matt vomited. Not just vomited. Spewed.

The contents of his stomach shot to the end of the bed.

"My God," Sarie said.

A nurse scrambled for a plastic basin. Another nurse grabbed for towels to clean away the vomit. Donna rushed to help her.

A doctor lunged for the cart beside the bed. Grabbing the syringes marked *Gentamicin* and *carbenicillin,* he injected them through Matt's IV line.

"He's already getting the Vancomycin," the doctor in charge of the ward said. "With these others, we ought to be able to attack whatever infection he's got." He frowned toward David. "How the hell you knew this would happen . . ."

"The Vancomycin's the important one. Keep giving it to him."

"We *have* been! You forced us to inject it on a regular schedule since you gave it to him last night! How did you know . . . ?"

Matthew vomited again.

Explosively. A white fluid streaked with red.

The nurse holding the plastic basin didn't catch all of it. Donna and the other nurse kept wiping the vomit from Matthew's sheets. Sarie rushed to help.

"Blood cultures," the doctor in charge of the ward said. "The lab. Find out what kind of infection he's got."

An assistant was already in motion. Inserting an IV needle into Matthew's left arm, he filled several vials with blood.

"Staph and strep," David said. "That's what the lab'll tell you."

The doctor frowned again toward David. "Not likely, since he's already covered for that. It could be any number of other bacteria. We don't know *what* the lab'll tell us. This is all a coincidence. The fever just happened to start when you said it would."

"Believe what you want. Just save my son!"

Matt vomited again.

"Another basin! Get another basin!" a nurse yelled.

David grabbed for one off a shelf.

The color of Matthew's skin was alarming, no longer pale but red, speckled with crimson spots: tiny hemorrhages beneath his skin.

With dull swollen eyes, Matt squinted toward the contents of the basin the nurse held. "White?" He groaned. "Why am I vomiting white?"

"That's the medication we've been giving you to coat your stomach." A doctor tried to sound reassuring but wasn't successful. "To help prevent ulcers from the chemotherapy."

"But it's streaked with . . . red." Matt gasped. "Am I throwing up *blood?*"

No one dared to answer.

David handed the nurse the empty basin, hurrying to remove the one Matt had filled. The exchange occurred just in time. Matt vomited again.

A doctor pivoted toward one of Matthew's IV stands, pressing buttons on a pump, increasing the flow of saline solution into Matt's body. "He's losing too much fluid. We've got to keep him hydrated."

Urgent voices overlapped.

"Blood pressure."

"Check it again."

"What's his temp now?"

The nurse who was helping Donna and Sarie clean the vomit from the sheets quickly reached for the computerized thermometer. At once she realized she couldn't put anything into Matthew's mouth. She groped into a pocket of her uniform, pulled out a standard thermometer, shook it, and wedged it under Matthew's right armpit.

Just then, the smell and sound unmistakable, Matthew's bowels let go.

David's arms and legs rippled with hot and cold rushes. His lungs heaved, making his mind spin. *No, please. Not now. I can't have another attack. Matt needs me.*

Added to his symptoms was a dizzying sense of déjà vu. In theory, he was witnessing these terrifying events for the first time, and yet he saw the chaos around him in double focus, as if this was the second time he'd been here. Each horror was occurring after he sensed it would. He'd seen it all before, endured it all before. From an impossible perspective, forty years from now on his deathbed, he relived hell.

15

Even before Matthew's bowels lost control, David reacted as if they already had. He grabbed towels off a shelf and raised Matthew's sheets. When what he expected to happen did happen, he experienced another eerie shift in time, not from the future into the present, but from the present into the past. For while he used a towel to wipe the excrement from Matthew, he couldn't ignore that what he did now for his fifteen-year-old son was exactly what he'd been accustomed to doing when his son was newly born. David's soul almost burst with love as he performed without disgust this most intimate of acts.

"I'm sorry, Dad."

"You don't need to apologize. You've no idea how glad I am to help you. I'll do anything to get you through this, to make you feel better. In fact, if there's a God, I started to do that, to help you, last night."

Matt's red face dotted with crimson formed a weak smile, almost the boyish grin David had seen on Matt in better times.

"I love you, son." David's throat ached so much it strangled him. He threw a soiled towel into a trash container and used another to continue wiping excrement from Matthew's hips.

"His temperature's up again." The nurse read a Celsius number, which David knew from experience was the Fahrenheit equivalent of a hundred and five.

More overlapping voices.

"Get that temp down."

"Ice. Wet towels."

"Compazine. Settle his nausea."

"Increase his saline IV. More fluid."

"Blood pressure?"

"A hundred and thirty over ninety."

"A little high."

"But not alarming. Easily explained."

"Yes, the trauma of his vomiting."

David threw a second soiled towel into a waste container. "You're right," he told the doctors. "A hundred and thirty over ninety isn't a problem. His blood pressure won't go any higher. But it'll go lower."

"*What?*"

David glanced toward a swirling clock on the wall. Somehow, more than an hour had passed. It was now 4:12.

"It'll go *lower*," David said. "I predicted the septic shock would hit at four-thirty-six. But the Vancomycin I gave him changed the schedule. His temperature rose five minutes later than I expected. So the shock will hit—"

"Five minutes later?" the doctor David had argued with at noon asked. "God help me, I almost believe you."

"Four-forty-one? Less than a half an hour from now? Is that what you're saying?" The doctor in charge of the ward stepped close. "For the record, I want to hear this. How low will his blood pressure drop?"

"Forty over twenty."

"Down from a hundred and thirty over ninety? In less than thirty minutes! Improbable!"

"How I pray you're right."

The doctor studied Matthew. "His vomiting's under control. His bowels have stopped voiding. I think we've checked whatever's wrong with him."

David leaned against the wall. "With due respect, you're mistaken. But just in case, will you phone Intensive Care? Tell them you might have to send down—"

"No!"

"Why not?"

"They'd want a reason, and I can't give them one! They don't just jump into action because an anxious father has hunches!"

"Then I'll phone them myself."

"You don't have authority."

"But what if I'm right?"

"Intensive Care is *always* ready!"

David stroked Matthew's feverish forehead. "So. With no other options, I guess we have to wait. Son, I know this is all confusing. Trust me?"

"You, Dad?" Matt grinned sickly. "When didn't I trust you?"

"When I told you not to ride your skateboard down a hill toward traffic."

Matthew breathed. "I could stop that skateboard on a dime."

"You listened, though. We never had to find out. So listen again. If something bad happens to you in the next half hour, don't be afraid."

"I won't need to?"

"You'll want to. But I'll be here to hold your hand. Depend on it. I'll do everything I can to help."

"Of course. You're my dad."

"Just don't be afraid. That's your job, the most important way you can help."

"Hang tough, right?"

"Yeah. Hang tough." David turned so Matthew wouldn't see him crying.

16

"It's four-thirty-six." A doctor turned toward David.

"Temp?" another doctor asked.

"Slightly down. A point above normal," a nurse said.

"Blood pressure?"

"Down. A hundred and twenty over eighty."

"Perfect."

"Not for him. He tends to run a little lower," the nurse said.

"The difference is too slight to be bothered about."

"Oh, there'll be a difference," David said.

"But your deadline's come and gone," another doctor said. "I told you, the first time was just a coincidence. He just happened to spike a fever when you said he would."

"And I told *you*, the Vancomycin I gave him delayed the schedule."

"I've had enough of this. We controlled his infection."

"No!"

"Everything's back to normal," the doctor said. "Now I've got rounds to make."

"Well, maybe we ought to . . ." The doctor from the Pediatrics Ward cleared his throat. "It wouldn't hurt. Just wait a few more minutes."

"And reinforce this man's delusion?"

"He's been right so far."

"Coincidence!"

"Just in case, though."

"Something's happening," a nurse said.

"What?"

"His pressure's down to a hundred."

"*Now* will you believe me?" David asked.

"Check it again," a doctor said.

"Down to ninety."

"No."

"I told you," David said.

"Eighty."

Matt vomited again.

"No!"

"Don't wait," David said. "Give him the dopamine."

"Dopamine? How did you know that's the drug we'd use to—"

"Raise his pressure? You wouldn't believe me! Give him the—!"

"Seventy."

"Do it!" David yelled.

"Can't you see we already are?"

Matt's body shuddered, convulsing.

175

"Sixty."

An intern injected the contents of a syringe into one of Matt's IV lines.

David exhaled. Panicked, he slumped against a wall. "And now we wait," he said. "And pray."

17

In David's nightmare, Matthew's plummeting blood pressure had not responded to the dopamine. The pressure had bottomed at forty over twenty, almost as low as it can get and still allow the body to maintain vital functions. Repeated injections of dopamine hadn't raised the pressure.

David had watched a frantic nurse crank up the end of Matthew's bed, raising his feet, helping his blood to circulate, trying to compensate for the devastating decrease in arterial pressure.

David had watched the doctor in charge of the ward phone Intensive Care. David, Donna, Sarie, a nurse, and a doctor had rushed Matthew's bed down hallways, into an elevator. Two floors below, they'd scurried with the bed down other hallways, into the ward that made the Emergency Ward seem primitive. As the document David had signed when Matt went into the Bone Marrow Ward so vividly put it, *You have a life-threatening disease. Within a year, you will surely die unless you receive exceptional treatment. A bone marrow transplant has serious risks, including infection.*

And, David mentally added, they don't rush you down to Intensive Care just to try out the machines.

In David's nightmare, higher doses of dopamine finally raised Matthew's blood pressure to a barely acceptable level of eighty over sixty. A team of trauma specialists waited in Intensive Care, and as soon as he arrived, the team snapped instantly into motion. David recalled no fewer than eight IV stands with two pumps on each injecting fluids and medications into his son.

But dopamine has plus and minus effects. It raises critically low blood pressure. However, to do so, it must stem the flow of blood to such crucial organs as the kidneys.

Matthew's kidneys shut down, stopped filtering poisons into the bladder. He needed a hole cut into his abdomen. A tube was inserted, through which fluid was poured in and an hour later drained out—to vent the poisons.

But now he was also on oxygen. If given long enough, oxygen poisons the lungs. Fluid accumulates. That fluid puts pressure on the heart.

Three organs in trouble. And that's not counting the remnant of the tumor in his chest, four missing ribs, and . . .

In David's nightmare, Matthew struggled against an oxygen tube crammed down his throat. Finally morphine had to be given, to put him to sleep, so he wouldn't yank the tube from his mouth.

Just before the tube was inserted and the morphine injected, the director of Intensive Care told David, Donna, and Sarie, "If you need to tell him something, now's the time. He might not come off the respirator."

Next to David, Sarie paled. "What does he mean, Matt might not come off the respirator?"

"It means"—David couldn't believe he was saying this—"Matt might die."

"Jesus."

18

What do you say to your son when the ultimate reality kicks him and you in the teeth? You've got five minutes to tell him the last words he might ever hear. Then, whether you said the right thing or not, you don't get another chance.

Your character, your upbringing, your *self* take charge.

Sarie chose to say, "I love you, Matt."

David chose to be practical. "Don't get panicked. Fear will increase your shock. Trust the system. I'll push these doctors to their limit. I promise, they'll do everything they possibly can."

Donna said . . . wise Donna . . . "Matt, you're a perfect boy."

A priest in the background said, "No, a perfect *man*."

Donna kissed her son.

The tube was inserted, the morphine given.

And that was the final communication.

Except . . . before drifting into a morphine stupor, Matt (unable to speak because of the oxygen tube crammed down his throat) pointed with determination toward letters on an alphabet board. His trembling finger wavered, spelling. The gist was clear.

Take this tube out. Need a root beer.

And then . . . *Die?* he spelled.

"We're doing our best," a doctor said.

Matt nodded. His eyelids fluttered. He slept.

The final communication.

Five days later, his injured lung collapsed.

But it reinflated, giving cause for hope.

Three days later, his heart became infected. His blood pressure plummeted, and this time nothing on earth or in heaven, no medicine, no prayers, would help.

19

Heartbroken, desperate for a second chance, David stared at the nurse taking Matthew's temperature.

"It's back to normal."

"Blood pressure?" a doctor asked.

"Up. Ninety over sixty-five."

"He's coming around," another doctor said.

"There." The doctor in charge of the ward turned to David. "A false alarm."

"Pressure—a hundred over seventy."

"I repeat," the doctor said.

"A false alarm? I watched you," David said. "You were afraid. But believe me, you couldn't have been as terrified as I was. What I did last night when I gave him the Vancomycin . . ."

"Was irresponsible."

"I saved my son's life!"

20

In David's nightmare, one of the bitterest ironies had been that as Matthew had worsened in Intensive Care, his recently transplanted bone marrow had started to multiply, producing healthy blood. Four days after the onset of his septic shock, Matt's white-blood count rose from zero to eight hundred. Not strong enough to fight infection but, under other circumstances, encouraging. As a rule, a white count of one thousand is considered the minimum safety level. The next time Matt's white count was tested, it had risen to sixteen hundred. And the next time, thirty-two hundred. When he died from heart arrest, his white count was over six thousand. If he hadn't contracted septic shock, his healthy blood would have permitted him to be released from the hospital the day of his death.

To be sure, there would still have been dangers. The devastating chemotherapy had temporarily destroyed his immune system. For several months, he'd have been susceptible to such normally nonlethal diseases as chicken pox, which he'd already had and acquired an immunity to, but which in his present weakened, nonimmune condition could have killed him. To guard against that danger, he'd have been forced to stay at home, his visitors restricted to those who had no illness and hadn't been exposed to any illness. Even then, his visitors would have been required to put on hospital face masks, just in case. When school started in the fall, Matt couldn't have attended but instead would have studied through correspondence courses.

But eventually, by Christmas, say, his immune system would have reestablished itself, and he could have gone out in public, resuming a normal life. In time, a brace would have been implanted in his chest to compensate for his missing ribs. Because he'd lost a third of his right lung, he'd have been short of breath on occasion but not enough to incapacitate him. A small price to pay for having survived.

Of course, he'd always have suffered the fear that his cancer had not been cured, that one day the tumor and its excruciating pain would return, but as the autopsy of David's nightmare indicated, no trace of malignancy was discovered. The devastating chemotherapy—possible only because of the bone marrow transplant—had been effective. The alien that Matt so loathed and wanted killed had been defeated.

Now, because Matt's septic shock had been averted, David's eerie déjà vu was restricted only to the no longer ironic increase of Matt's white blood count. Matt's vital signs remained at a normal level. His appetite increased. His only complaint was that he couldn't wait to go home.

"We'd like that, too," a doctor said, "but after what happened on Friday, we want to be cautious. It's been

181

a week now, Matt. You're doing fine. I think by Sunday, if you can be patient two more days, you'll be on your way."

Matthew raised his thumb in a victory signal.

David felt so elated he didn't care about the indignant looks a few doctors still directed toward him and the legal problems he'd be facing for having interfered with medical procedure. Yes, the hospital attorney had been called, but David didn't object. After all, parents can't be allowed to behave as if they're licensed to practice medicine.

Under normal circumstances anyhow. But since his nightmare, since David had awakened on his kitchen floor, nothing in his experience had been normal. His dizziness remained, though his heartbeat and breath rate were under control. His dizziness was more like floating, and periodically, when he closed his eyes, he still saw fireflies. At unusual moments, he'd turn toward Matthew's radio to reduce its volume, only to realize the switch was off, and yet he heard power chords. He and Donna continued to exchange what he felt were uncanny knowing glances, as if she understood the miracle that had happened and didn't dare break a spell by referring to it.

A spell. Precisely. David felt he was under a spell. None of what had happened—his panic attack, his struggle to convince the doctors, his 3:00 A.M. injection of Vancomycin, Matthew's recovery—none of it seemed real. He couldn't believe his luck. But he kept seeing fireflies. He kept hearing power chords. The need to stay close to Matthew became an obsession.

"Your son's doing fine," a doctor said. "Go home for a couple of hours. Get some rest."

"I'll go home when my son does."

The doctor frowned at David's haggard features.

"Hey, I'm okay," David said. "I'm just so glad he's alive I want to be near him. To . . . it's hard to explain . . . enjoy him."

"You explained it perfectly."

"Once he's home, I'll sleep for two days."

"You deserve it."

"So do my wife and daughter. None of us could have survived this without each other."

"All of us give you credit."

"No, Matthew deserves the credit. I don't know how he stayed so brave."

Then Saturday came.

21

Saturday. The day, in David's nightmare, when Matthew died in Intensive Care. David's dizziness made him feel that his feet floated off the floor. The fireflies brightened. The power chords intensified.

I'm losing my mind, David thought. That has to be it. I can't imagine another explanation. I'm cracking up from relief after six months of hell. But if David *was* cracking up, why, despite his sense of floating, did his thoughts seem so clear?

Something was wrong. From all appearances, not with Matthew. But *logically*. Something was wrong.

Okay, let's assume I fainted from running when I shouldn't have, when the temperature was too high, David thought. So I fell on the kitchen floor, had a nightmare that Matt would die, and woke up with the certainty I could save him because I knew exactly when and what would kill him. Does that make sense? Do you believe in precognition?

I've never believed . . . no, put it another way. I've never experienced it before.

A phone call you felt would come, and then it did?

On occasion. Coincidence.

But you did save Matthew's life. When the lab tests came back, they said his infection was due to strep and staph, and only Vancomycin—not the other two antibiotics you could have given—would have been effective against those bacteria.

Coincidence.

You don't believe that.

No, you're right. I don't believe that. I knew more than I could have.

Then what's your explanation?

As David's sense of floating increased, and the fireflies brightened, and the power chords nearly deafened him, he repeated, I'm going crazy! Or . . .

Yes, or?

Or I really am . . . !

Think it!

Dying forty years from now! And if I believe that, I belong in the Psychiatric Ward!

But if you did come back?

I won't consider it.

But if . . . ? There's a logical problem, right?

Yeah, a massive logical problem. I can't be in two places at the same time. If somehow I came back to change the past, then the future has to be changed as well. And I can't be dying forty years from now.

Then you either had a nightmare.

Or I'm dying in the . . .

Future? You mean the present, remembering the past, wishing with all your heart you could . . .

Change it?

But the past can't be changed. And on schedule, at 9:25 P.M. on Saturday, June 27, 1987 . . .

A chunk of debris from the dead staph and strep collected in Matthew's heart, plugged a major artery, and caused cardiac arrest.

It happened in an instant. The monitors attached to Matthew wailed. Sudden straight lines and zero readings.

And David's heart succumbed to its minor imperfection, the electrical blockage that had never bothered him. Till now. In the future. Which is to say, the present.

How long is an instant in eternity? Could it last ten earthly days?

David, who'd been hovering in the brilliant doorway, abruptly shot forward, at last released, finally at peace, no longer tortured by the greatest grief of his life.

His wife's fatal stroke in late age he could understand, though he missed her fiercely.

But his son's death at fifteen, his dear unlucky wonderful son, who embodied optimism, who exuded good

185

nature, who believed in being useful and could have contributed so much to a troubled world . . .

That death David had never adjusted to.

Until now. After forty years. At the instant of David's own death. With a vague sense of his beloved daughter weeping over his corpse, David rocketed through the radiant doorway. It seemed he'd been held in suspension, not for a microsecond but for agonizing days, until whatever held him back suddenly snapped and long-held pressure thrust him toward the mystery.

Toward fireflies and power chords.

Toward one of the fireflies rushing to greet him.

"Dad!"

The word was soundless.

Just as their loving embrace—so long postponed— was bodiless.

But David had no doubt . . .

"Son, I love you."

This was heaven.

Epilogue
THE REFRAIN OF
THE ANCIENT MARINER

1

Since then, at an uncertain hour,
That agony returns:
And till my ghastly tale is told,
This heart within me burns.

Thus we end as we began, with agony and compulsion. But what exactly have we been through? What did you just read? As I said at the start, this book is fact, with a layer of fiction. But how much of each? You've got a right to know.

Ninety percent of the events have been described as accurately as I can remember them. But memory, like reality (or perhaps the two are the same), can be illusory.

189

So to verify my recollections of the mostly factual events and conversations I've just described, I've asked several persons who were with me to read this manuscript and compare it to what they perceived, to make suggestions for alterations. Where appropriate for accuracy, those suggestions were followed. As a further test for accuracy, I referred to hospital records and a lengthy diary that my wife maintained throughout Matt's ordeal.

But what are the facts? Everything I described did happen—except for the obvious. I'm forty-four years old. Thus, at the age of eighty-four, I didn't have a deathbed vision that took me back forty years to try to save my son. I didn't anticipate the staph and strep that would give my son septic shock. I didn't become an amateur doctor, sneak into the hospital in the middle of the night, and give my son Vancomycin. I didn't head off the infection that sent Matt from the Bone Marrow Ward to Intensive Care, where after eight days of suffering he died from heart arrest. Everything that happens from the moment I wake up on my kitchen floor is invented. But everything in my nightmare during the fainting spell, all the specifics of the disaster I'm trying to avert, God have mercy, actually took place.

Examples.

On Thursday, one day before Matt contracted septic shock, did I foolishly run when the temperature-humidity index was one hundred and three and subsequently collapse on my kitchen floor?

Yes. But while in the book I forced myself to go to the hospital in response to a nightmare of precognition, in reality I staggered to bed and had to stay there

190

until the next day when I managed to get to the hospital two hours before Matt went into shock.

The initial medical explanation for my fainting spell was dehydration and an imbalance in the electrolyte components of my blood, i.e., loss of sodium and potassium. But fluids, sodium, and potassium didn't make me feel strong again and didn't take away my dizziness. In fact, when Matt was rushed to Intensive Care Friday evening, my disorientation worsened. On Saturday, after his kidneys failed and a hole was cut into his abdomen, a tube inserted, fluid poured in and drained out to vent his poisons, I had the unnerving sense that the floor was tilting. The flashing red numbers on his monitors made my heart rush in rhythm with them. When I leaned against a wall, it felt wobbly, as if I'd fall through it.

On Sunday morning, when Matthew's lungs began to accumulate fluid from too many hours on the respirator, I finally collapsed. The doctors, fearing I'd suffered a heart attack, rushed me to the Emergency Ward, where a team of specialists couldn't find anything seriously wrong with me. Stress and exhaustion, they diagnosed. But I realize now, because of subsequent medical treatment, that what I endured was a panic attack. In this book, I moved the panic attack back, from Sunday to Thursday, and made it a part of my imagined eighty-four-year-old dying vision.

The attack, I assure you, was real. Indeed, several months before, when Matt's chemotherapy kept producing no results, my wife experienced a similar attack. In her case, vomiting was an extra symptom. Dizzy, helpless, with a terrifying headache, rising blood pressure and heartbeat, she had to be rushed from a super-market to the Emergency Ward, where her chronic hypertension made the doctors suspect she was having a stroke. The results of tests made them reconsider their diagnosis and conclude that my wife had labyrinthitis, an inner-ear infection that upsets balance, produces nausea, and makes a victim so disoriented he or she swears that death is moments away. Valium was prescribed. For seven days, my wife had to walk with a cane. It is possible that my wife's labyrinthitis was a panic attack; I'll never know. But I certainly had one, and many others later.

Did Matthew's surgeons interrupt his eight-hour operation three hours into it to tell Donna and me that his tumor might be inoperable, that we had fifteen minutes to make a life-and-death decision: whether to close him up right now, allow him a relatively painless summer, and wait for his death in the fall, or whether to take out his ribs and however much of his lung, then go for the trauma of a bone marrow transplant, and hope he survived for a long productive life?

You bet that happened. Until that time, it was the worst day of my life, though there were many more horrible days to come.

Did I see fireflies in the darkness of my bedroom the night after Matthew died? Yes.

Did I experience a sudden inexplicable sense of peace when I entered the church the night before Matt's funeral, as if his spirit was telling me to grieve for myself but not for him because, in the firefly's word, Matt was "okay"? You bet.

But those two—I hesitate to call them "mystical"—sensations can be accounted for on a subjective level.

A skeptic would say that I saw what I wanted to see, that I felt what I needed to feel. I wouldn't argue. Till recently, I've always referred to myself as an agnostic, another word for hedging my bets, for saying I'm not sure about such ultimate matters as an afterlife and God. Not sure but not *un*sure either. Straddling the fence. Let's wait and see. God *could* exist. Maybe not.

The thing is, though, I did see the dove in the mausoleum. Reread my description of it in part one. It did behave in one of the three ways I mentally predicted. You'll have to take my word for those predictions. But the fact is, in front of twelve witnesses, the frantic dove suddenly settled to the floor as the priest completed the final rites over Matthew's ashes. The dove did allow me to pick it up. I did say, "And now I'll set Matthew free." I did carry the dove outside the mausoleum, and when I opened my hands, the dove (formerly panicked) did refuse to fly away. Until I thought, Dear God, I hope it isn't hurt. And at that point, a voice in my head said, "Dad, I'm all right," and the dove flew away.

You can doubt that my subjective reactions were mystical experiences. But what *isn't* open to doubt is that the dove was there and behaved as I've described. A chain of coincidences? Perhaps. But how many co-incidences do there need to be until you finally grant that something extraordinary, far beyond probability, took place? In my own case, I know I reached that limit. I started to slip off the fence. I began to wonder if the fireflies in my bedroom and my sudden sense of peace in the church were as subjective as a skeptic would claim. I took a step away from agnosticism toward . . .

Well, let's put it this way. I've got this friend. He

and his wife, after a yearlong lull in our relationship, showed up at the hospital the day after Matt contracted septic shock. They needed just one look at Donna, Sarie, and me to realize how helpless we felt, how much we required support.

In the worst of Matt's illness, I used to be so preoccupied I couldn't remember the last time I'd eaten or slept, and this was when I was having what I didn't know were panic attacks. My friend and his wife would force Donna, Sarie, and me to eat food they'd brought to the hospital. They'd compel us to take turns going back to their home, to lie down and try to rest. *Compassionate* is too weak a word to describe their behavior. (I hasten to add that some so-called friends who'd stayed in close contact in the year before Matt's illness fled from us as if we had the plague the moment they heard Matt had . . . dreaded word . . . could the disease be contagious? . . . we don't want our children to get it . . . dare we say it? . . . cancer.)

Anyhow, these friends whom we hadn't seen in a while, who suddenly showed up and exemplified the generosity of good samaritans, were with my family, my wife's sisters, and my brother-in-law when we left the funeral and went to the mausoleum to deposit Matthew's ashes. They were present during the incident with the dove, standing in the background, staring (I later learned) in astonishment.

Now understand, my friend is not religious.

But this is what he later told me. He turned to his wife and whispered, "Can you believe this is actually happening? Look at that dove. Look at how it waits while David picks it up. And look at how many people are seeing this. Thirteen people. It can't be we're all, so many, just imagining this."

Did you catch the error? I've mentioned several times that there were twelve of us in the mausoleum. Donna, Sarie, myself, two of Donna's sisters, my brother-in-law, the priest, the cemetery's sexton, and two representatives from the mortician. Plus my friend and his wife. Count them. Twelve.

But that day in the mausoleum, my friend saw thirteen. And to this day, no matter how often I count the witnesses with him, he still says he saw thirteen. And his wife who counted with him that day in the mausoleum agreed with him. Thirteen. A shadowy figure among the crowd, but a figure who wasn't there. Who or what? As my friends now say, "It's getting harder to be an agnostic."

I'm not claiming we saw a column of flame. And I'm not claiming my son was so special that if there is a God we received a sign. But something holy and unusual happened in that mausoleum. The priest who blessed Matthew's ashes had twenty years of experience in his vocation. At our home, at the gathering after the mausoleum, this seasoned professional of the spirit couldn't stop telling the hundreds of mourners about the dove. He based several sermons on it. Whenever I saw him afterward, he kept talking about the dove.

The mortician in charge of Matthew's disposition—another veteran, not of the spirit but of the soulless flesh—said in all her experience she'd never seen anything like, would never forget, the dove.

Make of the dove what you will. But I've been through hell, so now I'm willing to believe in the opposite. "Willing," I said. But I've got a good reason to grant that possibility. To be more specific, I've got a reason to *want* to believe. More about that later.

2

Why did I write this book? The truth is I didn't have a choice. It would have been impossible for me *not* to write it. I've never felt more compelled to put words onto paper. I guess you could call this a form of self-psychoanalysis. Something horrible happened to my son, and by extension to my wife, my daughter, and me. The worst thing. The most dreadful thing. I'm still trying to figure it out, to come to terms with it, to vent my emotions. In the months I've been writing these pages, I could barely see the keyboard because of the tears that blurred my eyes.

Then why not quit? Why torture myself?

Because even though it's torture, this book is also an act of love. In my mind, I'm still at the hospital, holding Matt's hand, stroking his forehead, trying to assure him there's hope. I can't give him up. He's been dead for months, and yet each day I study pictures of him (how I wish we'd taken more photographs). I caress his slippers. I strum his guitar. But my mental images of him are becoming cruelly less vivid. One day they'll be a blur, like my keyboard. So while he's still fresh in my mind, I write about him, even if the events I describe make my soul ache, because I want to make him permanent, if only on paper.

After his surgery, when Matt was told he still had a remnant of the tumor and would probably die, he murmured, "But no one will remember me." I promised he *would* be remembered, and as long as these pages exist and someone reads them, he *is* remembered.

But isn't that being merely sentimental?

In the first place, there's nothing wrong with being sentimental. That emotion and others such as compassion set us apart from animals. They make us human.

But in the second place, no, I'm not being merely sentimental. There are lessons here. Truths. They tumble through my mind.

3

Children are a gift. Throughout these pages, I've maintained that Matthew was a special child. His verbal and musical skills, his intelligence, his good nature were extraordinary. Everyone liked him. Everyone recognized his unusual potential. I truly believe that if he'd lived he would have made our world a better place.

Or is that fatherly pride? I don't want to nominate Matt for sainthood. He was special, but he wasn't perfect. He and I had "discussions" about curfews and other household rules. But yes, I was—am—proud of him. And that's my point. *Every* parent ought to have pride in his or her child, because *every* child is special, by virtue of being a child. From when Matthew was diagnosed in early January until he died in late June, for those six months, his mother, his sister, and I were with him almost constantly. Not always as a group, and not between treatments, when Matthew found the strength to go to school. But then his treatments lasted longer, and his sessions at school became shorter, and our family grew even tighter. For the last eight weeks of his life, Matt's home was the hospital, and one or all of his family was with him day and night.

When you think about it, the average parent sees his or her school-age child for an hour or two at most each day. In the morning, when the family's getting organized, and in the evening, when settling down at supper, then at bedtime. During the intervals, everyone goes a separate way. But we saw Matt *every* hour. During his final six months, and in particular, his final eight weeks, we spent more time together than an average family does over a lifetime. Maybe that closeness was a backhanded compensation for the pain and terror Matt (and by extension the rest of us) endured. Maybe Donna, Sarie, and I got to know Matt better than we ever normally would have, and to love him with greater intensity. Maybe six months or even eight weeks can be a lifetime. Maybe it's not how long but how well.

4

In the eulogy I wrote for Matt, I described how "I read in the newspaper about mothers who strangle unwanted newborn infants, about fathers who beat their children to death, while we wanted so desperately for our own child to live." I asked, "Why can't *evil* people suffer and die? Why can't the good and pure, for Matt truly was both, populate and inherit the earth?"

There's a writer I admire. Andrew Vachss. To date, his novels are *Flood* and *Strega*. Read them.

I admire him for two reasons.

First, because his sentences are strong; his stories make me turn the pages.

But the second reason I admire him is that he became a novelist out of frustration, because he wanted a broad audience to get the message of what he considers his *true* profession. He's an attorney who deals with child-abuse cases. Some time ago, I wrote a rave review of *Strega* for the *Washington Post.* He was kind enough to send me a letter of thanks, not for the review but for emphasizing the message of his books. "Not for my writing," he said, "but for my *work*." After Matt's death, he phoned to convey his sympathy.

"I can't tell you how sorry I am," he said. "Truly it breaks my heart. But for what it's worth, if this helps . . . I've seen so many dead battered children . . . at least your son had this privilege. He died knowing he was loved."

I started to cry but somehow kept talking. "Your days must be hell, dealing with . . ."

"These scum who treat children like sacks of garbage? No. My days are victories. I feel as if I save the lives of more children each year than most doctors do in emergency wards. Tomorrow I go to trial against a fourth-generation incest case, and man, I can't wait to put those perverts out of society. Abused kids are POWs. Establishing them with a decent family is like ending a war."

Child abuse.

Intolerable.

Unforgivable.

Children are precious, to be cherished. I always knew that. Believe me, that knowledge has been reinforced.

5

Cancer. I used to be afraid of it. Not anymore. Because it once was an unknown enemy. But now it's horribly familiar. And what's familiar isn't as fearsome as the unknown.

A few days ago, one of Matt's doctors came to visit. I told him what I was writing. I expressed my concern that someone afflicted with cancer might be advised not to read this book.

The doctor shook his head in disagreement. "Matt's cancer was rare, and it chose a rare site—a rib instead of an arm or a leg. As near as we can tell, though, we cured it."

"He died!"

"Because of an infection of a type that almost never happens. A biological accident."

"Whatever, he's still dead!"

"David, listen. Based on the autopsy results, I have to believe Matt would have survived. From the cancer. You'll hate me for saying this. Your son was unlucky. Rare cancer. Rare site. Resistant to chemotherapy. Finally responded. Shrank, but metastasized. Surgery got most of it. Chemotherapy combined with a bone marrow transplant got the rest of it, but a biological accident killed him. What we learned from Matthew's death takes us a step ahead in curing Ewing's sarcoma."

"What's that got to do with—!"

"Whether a cancer victim should read this book? Your son, God bless him, may have been the only victim, in this country, of that rare cancer in that rare site. And he stared it bravely in the face. He went all the way with it. Successfully. Except for the septic shock. If Matt could stare that rare cancer in the face, imagine the inspiration he can provide to victims of much more common cancers, of malignancies we usually *can* cure. He provides an example. If Matt could be brave, given the worsening complications he stoically accepted, maybe he'll show others how to fight their illness. David, you know we've had successes, even with Ewing's. You've spent six months in the cancer ward. You've seen patients go home."

"Some didn't."

"There are *no* guarantees. What I'm saying is, panic's an enemy too! But Matt didn't panic! So finish the book. And if civilians read it—not a doctor like me and a veteran like you—maybe they won't be so ignorant

201

about chemotherapy and how it's administered and why a patient goes bald and what the chemicals do and why and how and what and . . ."

So today I'll finish the book, and maybe some readers will find it frightening, but maybe other readers will learn.

6

But why did I write this book as I did, so a portion of it was fiction? In a paradoxical way, the fictional portions too are fact.

I never believed Matt would die. To his final hours in Intensive Care, I remained convinced that he'd survive. After his death, I still could not accept it. Sure, the doctors came out to the waiting room and told us he was dead. Donna and Sarie saw the body (I was on the verge of another panic attack, physically incapable of standing, of going into his room). They described how pathetically lifeless Matt's scarred, bruised corpse looked, finally out of pain.

"There must be a soul," Donna said, "because without it he didn't look the same. He just looked empty."

Donna explained how the Intensive Care staff prayed along with her and Sarie over Matthew's corpse. Then of course there was the autopsy, the cremation, and the funeral.

But even when we deposited the urn containing

Matt's ashes into the crypt, I still did not believe Matt was dead.

This isn't real, I thought. This can't be happening. It's a nightmare. I'll wake up, and Matt'll be fine. For days afterward, and especially the nights, I used to pray for the terrible hallucination of Matt's death to end. The only reason I was able to sleep is that I couldn't wait to wake up and discover Matt's death had been only a vivid nightmare.

Each morning as my consciousness focused, I'd feel a surge of hope, then realize that the nightmare hadn't ended, the hallucination hadn't faded, and I'd plummet back into despair. But still I'd keep saying, "This can't be real."

That was one of my reactions. Another was my utter conviction that if Matt's death impossibly *was* real, there had to be a way to reverse what had happened, to go back in time and save him.

I truly believed that. I thought if I concentrated hard enough I could turn the clock back. I spent many hours praying for a miracle, for a time warp, for a chance to leap into the past and somehow keep Matt alive. Throughout Matt's treatment, the doctors had given us detailed explanations about his disease and how they were trying to fight it. After Matt's death, the doctors gave us equally detailed explanations about what had killed him, about the staph and the strep and the septic shock. Every stage of Matt's treatment had been based on logic.

But a biological accident destroyed him. In case he developed a fever, a wide range of antibiotics was ready to be administered, and those antibiotics *were* given right away, the instant his fever started to rise. The infection *was* killed, but the shock the infection caused had been too strong for his weakened body.

In hindsight, the only way to have tried to save him (and I emphasize "tried" because there'd have been no guarantee the effort would have worked) would have been to administer the antibiotics *before* the fever started, to get a head start on the infection before it developed with the devastating swiftness of a fire storm.

But as a doctor explained, "Antibiotics are toxic when they don't have anything to fight. Bacteria can get used to them, so if an infection does occur, the antibiotics aren't effective." In other words, prematurely administered antibiotics might have made Matthew's condition even worse. Still, given the fact that Matt died anyhow, those antibiotics (if given before he seemed to need them) were all that might have saved him.

If. Might. Such despair-producing qualifiers. That's what cancer patients die from, "but ifs." If only this had worked or that hadn't happened. If. I believe that Matthew's doctors did everything in their power to try to save him. I understand how unorthodox it would have been for them to administer antibiotics before his symptoms demonstrated a need for that kind of treatment.

I'm not criticizing. I want to make that clear, and I also want to make it clear that parents of cancer victims shouldn't try to be doctors or think they know better than medical experts. It isn't even wise to go through medical texts, because those texts are often outdated (especially in terms of cancer research, which constantly develops new techniques of treatment).

But I keep telling myself this can't have happened,

it isn't real, Matt didn't die. And I keep telling myself those antibiotics were his only chance. So finally I wrote this book—to tell you what happened to my son, and at the same time to dramatize my sense of unreality.

Am I still in a faint on my kitchen floor? Has all of this been a nightmare? Will I wake up to discover that Matt didn't die and I didn't write this book?

I pray so. Or am I dying forty years from now, recalling the greatest loss of my life, still trying to find a way to bring Matt back? Anything's possible, because as far as I'm concerned the *im*possible happened to Matt.

That's what I meant when I said that even the 10 percent of fiction in this book is paradoxically true, because my fantasy dramatizes two phenomena of grief— the sense that it's all a nightmare, and the need to go back in time and make matters right.

My final scene, in which Matthew dies in 1987 while "David" dies forty years later and their souls as fireflies surge blazing toward each other, illustrates something else I said. I mentioned I'm falling off the fence of agnosticism. I'm starting to believe in God and an afterlife. *Because I need to. Because I so desperately want to see my son again.* Believing in God gives me a hope. Can faith be far behind?

7

Is there no pity sitting in the clouds
That sees into the bottom of my grief?

—SHAKESPEARE
  Romeo and Juliet

I've been told that the loss of a child you loved is among the worst agonies a human being can suffer. A subjective statement, of course, and I certainly don't want to get into any contests about grieving. My stepfather died eight years ago. That hurt me a lot. One of my wife's sisters died the following year, and *that* hurt a lot. Those were my only experiences of powerful grief. Until now. But those two painful losses can't compare to my present agony. I shudder at the thought that I might survive my wife. For the moment, though, let's grant the statement. The loss of a child you loved is among the worst ordeals a human being can suffer. The promise of youth destroyed. The potential for zest and goodness torn away. The unfairness of it all, and you miss the kid so much.

There have been days when I didn't think I could survive the pain. I contemplated suicide. What stopped me is that a month to the day after Matthew died, my daughter found the body of a friend who'd shot himself to death. He'd placed a towel beneath his head before he pulled the trigger. To minimize the blood. I couldn't put Sarie through more torture. I couldn't bear forcing her to attend the funeral of her father.

So I survive day by day, and the thoughts that help me are as follows.

206

8

The world is based on entropy, the messiness of the universe. Physicality is imperfect. Disintegration and random chance are the rule. If you have a good day, count yourself lucky. And if you wonder how God could cause something so devastating as the death of your son, you'd better rephrase the question, because God didn't cause your son's death. The chaotic nature of the world did. God is perfect. The world is not.

You could say that God should have done a better job when creating the world. But Perfection can't create Itself. It can only create a lesser version. You could also say that God should have intervened to prevent the death of your child. But that would be a miracle, and no one has a right to expect a personal miracle.

I remember praying for a miracle. When Matt was close to death, I tried to make one of those bargains that Elisabeth Kübler-Ross refers to in her books about the nature of death and dying. But I couldn't think of a reason for God to help *me* instead of all the other troubled souls in this world. I finally thought I'd found an argument that couldn't be refused.

Dear God, I prayed, just as you're supposed to be a father to me and to love me as your son, so please identify with the love I feel for *my* son. Please help my son, because *Your* son is asking *You*.

The prayer didn't help. But I'm not bitter that it wasn't answered. After all, I was trying to make a deal, and maybe that's the wrong thing to do, to try to make a deal with God. Maybe if I'd believed in Him totally before Matt got sick, maybe if I'd had faith in Him to start with and not just now, Matt would have lived.

Well, that's another issue. The miracle did not occur, and God neither caused nor took away my son's cancer, because the nature of the universe He created doesn't permit His intervention. That's why there's a heaven, I want to believe, because it's a goal, a step up from the chaos of earth.

9

If you believe in Original Sin, you understand why the world's imperfect and why God tests us instead of intervening.

But if you *don't* believe in Original Sin . . .

Compassion.

I've said that Matt believed in the value of good nature. If everyone every day showed good nature to everyone else, most of society's problems would disappear. Recently an editor acquaintance called me and paraphrased a quotation from a book whose title he no longer remembered. "From the start of human history, there's been so much pain and suffering the stars should have stopped in their tracks." My acquaintance ought to know. He's suffered twice my tragedy. *Two* of his children have died. I don't know how he keeps going. But my acquaintance (I keep using that word because I see him but once a year, and that's what impressed me— he wasn't a *friend* and yet he was phoning me) spoke only briefly about his own tragedies. He said he was calling because he'd heard about *my* son's death, and he wanted to tell me how deeply it filled him with sorrow.

Compassion. If you think about it, every person you know, every friend, every stranger, in every building you pass, will one day (and perhaps even now) have a devastating personal loss. My acquaintance exemplified what we have to do. Show our compassion. We have to say, "I'm filled with sorrow for what you're suffering."

We have to weep for the pain of our fellow mortals. You've probably seen those bumper stickers that ask, "Have you hugged your kid today?" You bet. And our fellow sufferers. The letters of consolation my family received, not only from friends but sometimes from strangers, were powerfully helpful. They showed my wife, my daughter, and me that we weren't alone, that someone cared, that shoulders were there to lean on.

Lately I've found that I've been hugging people a lot, and until Matthew's death, I wasn't what you'd call a touchy person. I hug them impulsively, and it seems to help me and *them* feel better about the day, about persisting in this tenuous universe.

"Life is suffering," I said in Matt's euology, quoting the first of the great truths of Buddha. Let's face up to that and show the best of our human qualities—not intelligence; I think that'll doom us, if nuclear weapons and worldwide pollution are any evidence of our stupid cleverness. Not intelligence but compassion.

What else have we got to depend upon except each other? If someone you know has pain, tell him or her you're sorry. Don't keep a distance. Be human.

10

There's another aspect of grief I need to talk about. Its physical effects. I've described my collapse while Matthew was unconscious in Intensive Care. I've dramatized my experience in the Emergency Ward, where cardiologists and neurosurgeons tested me and finally explained that I'd succumbed to stress and exhaustion—a frightening condition, though I hadn't yet learned that "fear" exactly described my symptoms.

Three weeks after Matthew's death, at nine o'clock on a Wednesday night, I sat in a La-Z-Boy chair to watch a TV program I'd been anticipating, an episode in a brilliant thriller from Britain, called "Edge of Darkness." I use the world "thriller" in a qualified sense. At the beginning of this episode, there was nothing "thrilling" going on. Scenes were being set, characters established. But the show was a distraction, and I was grateful for anything that might help take my mind off Matthew's death.

Suddenly I felt a tingle in my feet. In hot and cold rhythms, it rushed up my legs, soared through my abdomen, and reached my heart. As I've said, I'm a runner. Because of that physical conditioning, my normal heartbeat is sixty. At once, it beat faster. I checked my pulse. It had risen to ninety. With equal abruptness, it raced beyond my ability to check it.

I hyperventilated. I convulsed. I felt as if I'd just run a fast five miles. My guess is my pulse was now a hundred and fifty. And then the spasms hit my head, and as Donna raced across the room to try to help me,

I managed to say, "I'm having a . . . heart attack. I'm . . . going to die."

You can't imagine my terror, and you can't imagine how quickly this incident occurred. A minute ago, I'd been fine. Now I was heaving in my chair and sure I was dying.

As quickly, the spasms dwindled. My heart rate went down. My breathing returned to normal. But I was so shaken by the experience I couldn't function for two days.

That's when I decided I needed more medical advice. Through the grace of a doctor friend, I was able to interrupt a cardiologist-internist's hectic schedule and be examined. This kind man took three hours to check me thoroughly. To be prudent, he even ordered sophisticated heart tests known as echo-and-sonograms. When he concluded, he told me I was one of the healthiest persons he'd ever examined.

"No, there's something wrong with me," I insisted. "My head. I think I need a CAT scan. Maybe I've got a tumor. Maybe if . . ."

The doctor, who knew I wouldn't mind his sense of humor, said, "Oh, I think you've got something in your head all right. But a CAT scan isn't going to find it."

"You think I'm nuts?"

"I think you've been having classic panic attacks. You need to see a psychiatrist."

Now to me, a psychiatrist meant psychoanalysis, and since I'm a fiction writer, I worried that he might misinterpret my ability to imagine and suspect I was having delusions. But the result was quite the contrary. The psychiatrist listened for ninety minutes as I babbled about my supposed heart condition and my son's death, and finally he told me with compassion that he concurred with the cardiologist's opinion. I was suffering classic panic attacks. In lay terms, my emergency defense system—exemplified by my adrenal gland—had worked so hard before and after Matthew's death that it wouldn't turn off. Now for no apparent reason but with obvious subconscious prompting, it was kicking into gear when there wasn't an emergency.

So here I am, on four tranquilizers and a sleeping pill each day. I haven't had further panic attacks, though I do hyperventilate on occasion; but I'm learning how to subdue that. If you're suffering from grief and you've endured the symptoms I just described, don't assume they're panic attacks. Don't be an amateur physician. Have a medical exam (because your heart might indeed be infirm). But if the diagnosis does turn out to be panic disorder, your condition *can* be controlled. You'll still grieve. There's no cure for that. But at least you won't have panic to add to your terrible sorrow.

11

Yesterday my son's principal physician came to see me. He brought Matt's final autopsy report. It proves that the fantasy you just read isn't possible. Even if I did have precognition, I couldn't have saved my son. He was sicker than I feared. The debris from the dead bacteria that plugged his heart and killed him was only one of many things wrong with him. The debris had also plugged an artery to his brain, causing major cerebral damage. If Matt had survived the septic shock, he'd have been mindless at best. In addition, he had fungal and yeast infections throughout his body. They would have been fatal. As well, a brain aneurysm he'd had from birth could have ruptured and killed him at any time.

But most significant of all, the final autopsy, on a microscopic level, revealed that Matt's cancer wasn't cured. Malignant cells lingered on his spine. At this moment, my wife, my daughter, and I would be back with him in Intensive Care. But now, in addition to suffering indescribable pain, he'd have been paralyzed, no cure possible, the only mercy death.

My prayer was answered. Dear God, just as You're supposed to be a father to me and to love me as Your son, so please identify with the love I feel for *my* son. Please help my son, because *Your* son is asking *You*.

Matt died as best as possible. The worst, yet the best. Because at the moment what I formerly thought was the worst would be only the start of something far more horrible: a slower, more painful death.

I grieve. How much it hurts. But I'm at peace. Because I'm convinced at last that my son was doomed. *Nothing* could have saved him.

But Father . . .

God . . .

It hurts.

12

. . . Winter is come and gone,
But grief returns with the revolving year.

—PERCY BYSSHE SHELLEY
  "Adonais"

Cycles. Circles. Dates. Numbers. Anniversaries.

On November 9, 1977, when Matthew was six, in the midst of an evening birthday party, Donna suffered a miscarriage. She lost what would have been our third child. This child had not been planned, but we anticipated it lovingly. I made two urgent calls—to Donna's doctor, who told us to rush to the hospital, and to a friend, who agreed to race to our house and allow Matt's birthday party to continue. Ironically, this friend was also present when I picked up the dove in the mausoleum after Matt's funeral.

The miscarriage occurred when the fetus was three months old. We never asked what sex it was or what caused its spontaneous abortion. But thereafter, whenever Donna and I celebrated Matthew's birthday with him, we also mourned for the unknown child who did not survive gestation.

Now on November 9, which is rapidly approaching, we'll mourn twice-over, for that unknown child and for a son we knew so well and will forever miss.

June 27, 1987. The date of Matthew's death. Since then, on the twenty-seventh of each month, we light a candle at 9:25 P.M., the moment he left us. Christmas will be hard. So will New Year's, and Thanksgiving will be most bitter.

Dates and cycles. Mental tombstones.

But this is what I most dread.

Last winter was mild here in Iowa. It snowed almost never. But in early January, when Matthew was diagnosed and received his first chemotherapy, I remember one evening how I stared out a window of his hospital room. Outside, the arc lights reflected off glimmering snow. I turned to Matt, who'd just finished vomiting, and told him, "It's snowing."

He murmured, "Yeah, I bet it's pretty."

"You always liked snow. Remember how we used to walk in it and build snowmen."

"I wish I could build one now."

"You will. Next year. We're in this together. We'll see you through this. Next year we'll walk in the snow."

"Can't wait,"

"Me neither," I said.

But Matt's not here now, and I'm still waiting for that first snow.

That will be the hardest time. Not November 9, or the twenty-seventh of each month, or Thanksgiving, or Christmas, or New Year's. No, that first snow will be the worst. But as hard as I'll have to force myself, I'll walk in it and build a snowman.

I'll try to believe in God. I'll try to have faith that I'll see my son again. I'll remember the sudden peace I felt in church that night before his funeral. I'll recall the dove in the mausoleum. I'll pretend I hear Matt's guitar, its power chords blasting from his bedroom window.

And as the snowflakes melt on my face, blending with
my tears, I'll imagine those flakes—
they'll glisten from streetlights—
I'll imagine those snowflakes are fireflies.

June 28—September 4, 1987